love

lessons

je rowney

the lessons of a
student midwife

BOOK TWO

Also by this author

Charcoal
Derelict
Ghosted

THE LESSONS OF A STUDENT
MIDWIFE SERIES:

Life Lessons

Copyright © 2020 JE Rowney

Chapter One

By the beginning of October, Zoe and I are desperate to get back to Tangiers Court. All we have been able to talk about for the past week is coming back, starting our second year at Wessex University, and settling back into our life here. We could have returned sooner; the house has been empty, waiting for our arrival.

One day, a couple of weeks into August, Zoe drove us up here. We spent the afternoon in Blackheath's cafe, drinking latte (me) and mocha (Zoe) and dreaming of the start of the new academic year. We passed down the street and paused for a few moments outside number twenty-one. Our home. We both had our keys with us, but we didn't stop, we didn't go in. What would be the point? It wouldn't be the same. No lectures to prepare for. No Luke.

At the beginning of the holidays, Zoe talked about Luke non-stop. It's become better over time, but only because she has learned to stop herself. I find it funny now; I

1

don't mind all that much. Not really. It's not like I have anyone to rabbit on about. I love her romantic streak; I don't think I have one of my own. Perhaps when I meet the right person everything will change.

So now, here we are.

If there was one take away learning point that I picked up moving in here last year, it was that carrying several bags full of clothes and general bits and pieces down the road is hard work. I learned a lot of other things too, of course. I learned that anxiety is a beast, but that every so often I can tame it. I learned that other people can appear to be challenging (to put it politely), until you take a step back and see the bigger picture. I learned that I can do things that I never thought I would be able to achieve. Now I'm back, and I want to learn more.

I've borrowed my mum's suitcase on wheels, and I'm pulling it up the street towards Tangiers Court. It's an ugly blue plastic monstrosity, but at least my arms aren't aching. Zoe has plumped for a rucksack. Well, a rucksack and two suitcases; she doesn't know the meaning of travelling light.

"You want a hand with some of that?" I ask her.

She shakes her head, but she pauses again, redistributing the weight of her cargo.

"No, no. It's fine. We're nearly there now."

I stop beside her and reach out to take the smaller of the cases.

"What have you got in this one anyway? It weighs a tonne."

"You know. Stuff. The stuff you always borrow from me. You've probably only got less clothes because you borrow half of what you wear from me!" She's smiling when she says it.

I wish it were true. Zoe is a slim size 8, and I'm a curvy 14 on a good day. She does have a few sweet sweaters and cardigans that I have maybe, possibly been known to squeeze into, but I could never borrow most of what she wears. We are different shapes, different sizes, but so what? She's my best friend. Always has been, always will be.

"I wish!" I grin back at her and hoist the case up clumsily on top of mine. It forms a double-decked stack that I can just about

3

pull with the rickety metal handle that rises from the top of Mum's case.

"I should have got one of those," Zoe says.

"Next year!" I say, but I know she will have forgotten by then, and I will forget to remind her.

I pull the luggage behind me, but Zoe's case wobbles from precariously on its unstable foundation, and I can't trust it to be out of my sight. Instead, I turn the cases around gently, get behind them and - very carefully - start to push.

"I hope we are here before him," she says.

I know who she means, of course.

"You've waited all this time to see Luke, and now you don't want him to be here?"

"I want him to be here *soon,* but I want to get changed, freshen up, make myself look human." She gestures at her hair as though it's a wild bush. She's wrong though. It's perfect.

"You look amazing already!" I say. She does. Her flame-red hair is brighter than ever in the Autumn sunlight. Her skin is

4

clear, and slightly less pale than usual after sitting out in the sun over our break.

She brushes the compliment away.

"Did he say when he would be back?" I ask.

We started off a group chat last year for important conversations such as "Pick up some more toilet roll when you're near Wilko x" or "If you don't get out of bed soon, you're going to miss Cooking Queens xxx". I haven't paid much attention to the conversation over the summer, but every now and again I see a notification pop up that Zoe or Luke have added a message. Not like she couldn't just text him privately, of course, but I guess using the group chat must have felt threatening.

"Today," she says. "He didn't say when though."

It's around three o'clock now. Luke lives in Leeds when he is not at uni. It's a good four and a half hours away; I doubt he would be here much earlier than this.

Nonetheless, as we approach Tangiers Court, and Zoe puts her hand into her pocket to fish out her key, I put my hand out to stop her.

5

The door is wide open.

"Hello?" Zoe calls in.

She drops her remaining case in the hallway and starts to shrug the rucksack off her shoulders. There are two angry marks on her skin where the straps have been digging into her. I knew it was too heavy.

I stand behind her, peering into the house.

"Luke?" I shout. "Are you home?"

The door to the living room is closed; the door ahead of us, that leads to the kitchen - the one we have never once closed since we moved in last October - is also shut.

There's someone in there though.

"Luke?" I call again.

Zoe turns and whispers to me. "I'm sure it's fine. It must be Luke."

I shrug. It's broad daylight. I can't imagine that anyone would have broken in, left the front door open and decided to raid our very empty kitchen.

I lean the stacked cases against the wall, with the intention of walking down the hall. I've taken two steps before both cases

6

tumble to the ground in a clattering crash.

Behind the frosted pane of the kitchen door, I see a shape moving. A six-foot-tall shape reaches for the handle and opens the door.

It's not Luke.

"Er, hi?" It's not a question, but the way it comes out of my mouth definitely makes it sound like one.

"Hello," the man says.

The three of us stand in the narrow hallway, looking at each other.

He's holding a knife, thick with a blob of peanut butter. I can't seem to take my eyes off it.

After what feels like an age, Zoe says, "We, er…we live here."

He nods and licks the peanut butter off the steel. When he has finished, he says, "Good."

I wonder for a moment if he is not English, or at least if he doesn't speak English, if it isn't his first language. His complexion appears to be that of a fairly standard Englishman, with pale peachy skin; there's nothing about his looks that would back up my suspicion. I'm only on guard because he is not talking to us.

Zoe and I look at each other.

"I live here too," he says.

"Oh," I say. "Oh, right. Yes. The spare room."

"Not anymore," he says. "My room now."

He can speak English after all. He is English. He doesn't appear to have a lot to say though. His tone is flat, and I wouldn't exactly call it friendly.

"Right," I say.

We stand silently again until the awkwardness begins to overwhelm me.

"I'm Violet. This is…"

"I'm Zoe." She holds out her hand to him in an excruciatingly uncomfortable motion. He passes the butter knife to his other hand and shakes hers. After she lets go I notice her subtly wipe her hand onto her skirt. I decide not to offer mine.

"Carl."

Carl. A man of few words. Our new housemate.

Last year Tangiers Court felt fun, it felt spacious, it felt like home. I have only been back for ten minutes and I'm already starting to feel the change. I'd hoped that the spare room would remain empty, but at the back of my mind I suppose I knew that it was too much to ask. We had a good year here, Luke, Zoe, and me. This year though? Who knows?

Carl turns and goes back into the kitchen without saying anything else, leaving Zoe and I standing in the hallway, equally at a loss for words.

Chapter Two

When Luke arrives later the same evening, Zoe and I are sitting in the living room, in our usual positions. The final chair, the one we used to joke belonged to Andrew, our imaginary fourth housemate, remains empty. The best thing about Andrew was that he didn't exist. We could use him as an excuse for all the things that we wanted to do (like order takeaway because it was his turn to make dinner) or didn't want to do (usually the washing up or the cleaning). Now we have Carl, and we are going to have to learn how to fit around a real person.

As soon as Zoe hears the front door opening, she looks at me with a huge grin on her face. She spent the majority of our first year here crushing on Luke and not actually doing anything about it. Perhaps it is finally time for her to act on her feelings. The door to the living room is open, and Luke pops his head in.

"Ladies!" He sounds as excited to be back as we are.

"Luke!" There's no holding back.

10

Zoe jumps to her feet and runs to launch a big hug at him.

I bring myself to a standing position and offer my arms out too. "Hey! Welcome back. Was your drive okay?"

"It feels longer every time," he says.

"Yeah, same," Zoe smiles. Then, in a hushed, conspiratorial tone she says, "Someone has moved into Andrew's room!"

Luke affects a look of feigned shock. "Have you told Andrew? Someone should let him know!"

Zoe pats him softly. "Silly! It's good to see you."

He pauses, then says, "You too."

I get a little warm flutter in my chest. I really hope they don't leave it too long before one or the other of them makes a move. It's like waiting for an inevitable storm to break, but a good storm, the kind you are waiting for when the days have been long and hot, and you need the relief of rain.

"Let me get this stuff upstairs and I'll come and have a drink with you. I assume you're not going to have a repeat performance of your first night here last year."

Zoe laughs. I'm sure she would rather that he forgot how drunk, and how sick, she was.

"Not for me, thanks," she says.

"I'll make us a brew." I smile, and head towards the kitchen, leaving Luke and Zoe standing together for a few more minutes, alone, before Luke goes up to his room.

Ten minutes later Luke comes back downstairs and sits on the sofa next to Zoe.

"Did you see him?" I ask, handing Luke his coffee.

"Thanks Vi. Andrew? I mean, Carl?" Luke says.

"Uh huh." As we didn't mention his name I assume that Luke *has* met our new housemate.

"Yeah," he says. "He was complaining that you two had the best rooms and wondering why I let you get away with it."

"What?!" Zoe almost knocks the mug out of Luke's hand, as she jumps upright. "He never said that."

Luke's expression remains

12

unchanged.

"He did say that?" Zoe is wide-eyed. "Wow! We have been here a year and he walks in and…"

She brings the sentence to a close as we hear the sound of footsteps on the stairs.

We all look at each other. The atmosphere here has certainly changed.

The footsteps come to a stop outside the living room, and Carl looks in.

"I'm going to head down to the union tonight," he says. "Any of you want to come?"

If we say no, we are not going to make a particularly friendly first impression on our new housemate. On the other hand, I really do not want to go out and drink. I want to stay here, watch Netflix, and catch up with Luke. I want to start settling back into the life we had last year, the life that I have missed so much over the summer break. I want things to get back to normal, and with Carl here, I'm no longer sure that things are going to be the same.

"Not tonight," Luke says. "Sorry mate. We are fuddy-duddy housemates, I'm afraid. You'll find us with our hot chocolate and slippers by nine o'clock most nights."

I know Luke is trying to be friendly and joke with Carl, but the look that Carl gives him is neither friendly nor joking.

"Sure," he says. He looks to Zoe, and then to me. "I suppose the same goes for you two?"

"You're welcome to join us in here," I say, by way of a compromise.

He nods slowly, but his expression doesn't change.

"Sure," he says again, in the same flat tone. "Well, see you later then, guys."

With that, he is gone, out of the front door and off to the bar.

The three of us sit and look at each other.

"That was awkward." Luke says exactly what all of us are thinking.

"It must be difficult coming into a house where the other people know each other," I say. "What was it like for you last year? Zoe and I were already here, best friends all of our lives…"

"But Zoe broke the ice by throwing up and passing out on the floor," he says, and gives Zoe a cheeky wink.

14

Zoe raises her eyebrows and makes an over-the-top pouty face.

"Maybe we should have gone with him." The other two look at me in unison. "Okay, okay, I know," I say.

I'd expected us to have a chilled night, chatting about our summer holidays. Even though I thought that someone might possibly move into the empty room, I didn't think it would cause this much friction.

"It's early days," Zoe says. "Give him the chance to settle. We got used to Luke, didn't we?"

"I thought it was I who got used to you two. Well, I got used to Violet, at least. I don't think I will ever get used to the girl who leaves her tights hanging over the shower rail to dry."

"It's the best place for them!" Zoe protests. I'm starting to feel like maybe I should have gone out with Carl and left them to it.

I clear my throat. "How was summer?" If I don't bring the conversation around I'm going to end up going to my room.

"It's never particularly sunny in

Yorkshire, but there were a couple of days when it didn't rain." He settles back onto the sofa.

"We've been on the beach most days," Zoe says, "but you wouldn't have liked it. It was packed."

"The nearest beach to where I was must be an hour and a half away. Perhaps I should have stayed here."

"We did come past Tangiers Court once," I say, and Zoe throws me a sharp look. I don't know why she wouldn't want me to tell him that. It's not like he was in the house. "We went for coffee at Blackheath's and then...well, we didn't come in."

"I missed it too," Luke says. "I missed you too."

"And you," says Zoe.

The two of them look at each other for a few seconds before Zoe breaks eye contact.

"Anyone remember what episode of Scrap House we were up to?" She points the remote control at the TV and forces her attention away from Luke. Her face is glowing red though, and I'm sure he must have noticed it too.

16

Chapter Three

I've kept in touch with my closest course mates over the summer break, but it is still a great feeling when I see Sophie, Ashley and Simon on our first day back. Their out of term addresses are scattered across the country, so none of them have seen each other over the break either. Sophie and Ashley have a house share together this year with a couple of students from the nursing course, so they have had time to catch up before this morning at least.

I love learning, and I love my lectures, but I know that on the first day of our modules we will be given our assignments for the term. It's a bittersweet feeling to be back. Our unit guides give us an overview of what we can expect to cover during the term. I like to look at each of the sessions and look forward to each topic we will be taught about. At the back of the document for each module is an overview of the assessment, what we have to submit for the course and when. I would rather be given that information later down the line, closer to the deadline time. I want to enjoy learning, without thinking that I have to prepare to be assessed on what I have learned. At least this term there aren't going to be any exams.

Last year, the focus of our modules was on learning about the normal parameters of maternity. We were taught about the fundamentals, and how to assess and recognise deviations from them. This year we move on to look at more complex issues, pathophysiology and medicines management. Midwifery isn't just about delivering babies, taking blood pressures, and feeling women's bellies. Being a midwife means bearing a huge weight of responsibility.

We have six weeks of classes before we start our first placements of the year. Today's first lecture is an introduction to the new module, 'Altered Health in Pregnancy and Childbirth'.

"You all came back," the lecturer says, as she looks around the room. "Twenty-three out of twenty-three. That's impressive. When I did my training, two of the girls dropped out over the summer

18

holidays because they were pregnant. One of the occupational hazards of working in this profession, I'm afraid."

There's a low rumble of laughter. I can't imagine getting pregnant on this course, I would be surprised if I even had time to have a relationship.

"I'm Sarah. I work here part-time, and for the rest of the time I have an independent midwifery practice. I work with two other midwives, and we can have a talk about independent midwifery at some point."

A quick, quiet buzz passes around the room as the class turn to each other and make their hushed, excited comments. I hadn't even considered that there were options outside of working in a hospital, in the NHS. It's easy to assume that most babies are born in hospitals and so that's where I should work. I have another two years to think about what I want to do, and where. Two years. That's not long at all.

"This term, we are going to start exploring some of the things that can go wrong in pregnancy, or at least could go wrong if we don't identify them early and take the appropriate action. We will look at pathophysiology in this module, and your other module for this term will explore your role as public health practitioners."

Public health. I barely understand what the phrase means. I'm sure that I will before too long.

"Patho-physio-logy." Sarah says as she writes the word on the board, split into three component parts. "The Greeks have it all backwards, of course. 'Logos' means 'the study of', 'physio' – 'nature', and 'pathos' translates as 'suffering'. Essentially, it's the study of where suffering originates, but more simply pathophysiology is about looking at abnormalities and changes in body functions."

I write it down on my notepad, hoping that it will make more sense to me later. Sometimes it all sounds far more technical that it needs to. It's about when things go wrong. That's all I need to know for now.

Sarah is still talking. "This module will have a written assessment, but during the course I will also expect you to submit formative reports on the topics that we cover so that I can check that you are on the right track."

I thought the workload was steep last year. Now I will have placements, assignments for the other module, an essay to write for this, and all that extra work. It feels overwhelming already and we haven't even begun yet. I can feel my palms begin to sweat, and my attention is drifting. I try to focus and bring my thoughts back to the room.

Ashley, sitting to my right, has written on a piece of paper in the front of her new A4 pad, and she pushes it towards me. "At least there are no presentations this year," she has written, and followed it with a crudely drawn smiley face.

I'd almost forgotten how much I struggled at the start of last year. By repeating the process of preparing and presenting in front of the class, the process that caused me so much stress and anxiety at first, I managed to overcome my fears and gain skills that I never thought I would be able to. I had to be part of a group presentation every week, and I went from being terrified to being almost competent. If

I were asked to stand at the front of the class and deliver a presentation now, as long as I had time to prepare it properly, I think I could get up there without any fear at all. Of course, that's not what is being asked of me this term. Now I will need to channel my time into writing reports: less scary, but less interesting. It's not that I found being terrified *interesting*, but I actually did start to enjoy myself once I overcame my initial fears. That doesn't mean that I have even got started on overcoming my anxiety though. I'm not going to escape it that easily, I know.

I give Ashley a smile, flick my eyes over to check that Sarah isn't looking in our direction and I write on the pad, below Ashley's message.

"So much work though."

I draw a circle, dot in the eyes, and draw a downturned mouth. It seems that we even add emojis to written words nowadays. I'm so used to conveying my feelings, or at least stressing my meaning, with the tiny pixel pictures.

Ashley forms a tight-lipped grimace and mouths, "Ugh." She's so smart though,

I'm sure it doesn't bother her in the slightest.

"I'll be expecting a report from you every fortnight," Sarah says. "You can choose any of the pathophysiologies that we discuss to base your submissions on. You might want to reflect upon something you have experienced in practice. How many of you have met a woman with pre-eclampsia?"

Everyone in the class raises a hand, without exception.

"How many of you cared for someone with gestational diabetes?"

There are fewer hands lifted this time.

"I'm sure you can all think of someone you encountered over the past year whose pregnancy was not straightforward. It is our role to identify those deviations as soon as possible and take the appropriate action. We have to know what signs to look out for, what they may mean, and how we should respond. We need to know when we should refer women for further help, support or treatment."

I feel like that is what I try to do for

myself too. I watch for signs that my anxiety is building, I try to be aware of when my heart starts to race, when my mouth dries up, when my mind begins to lose focus. What I tend not to do is ask for help. Perhaps that is where I am going wrong. My thoughts are wandering now, but not in an anxious way. I'm starting to wonder whether I should try to take a hold of my own pathophysiology. How can I help other people when I can't even help myself? I bottled an exam and stressed about so much last year. I've struggled with my anxiety for such a long time, perhaps now it's time I did something about it.

This module might mean a lot of coursework but reflecting on other people's health may help me to think about my own.

Chapter Four

At the end of the third week back at Tangiers Court, life seems to be pretty much the same as it was last year. Luke, Zoe, and I spend most evenings together chatting and watching television. Sometimes Luke goes out with his course mates, and it's just the two of us. Apart from crossing paths sometimes in the kitchen, I have hardly seen Carl. We may as well have kept Andrew as our fourth housemate, although I'm sure the landlord is happy that he now has a real-life paying tenant.

This evening, Zoe and I have been home from uni for about half an hour. She's in her room and I've just made coffee. It's coming to the end of October, but the evenings have been warm this week. Our plan is to sit out in the garden until the sun goes down and we get too cold to stay out any longer. I pick up our mugs, and with one in each hand, I use my butt to push the back door open.

I nearly drop the two steaming cups as I see Carl sitting at the little white metal table. It's almost like seeing a stranger or an intruder, his presence is so unexpected.

He looks up from his phone and sees me almost stumble. Still, he doesn't speak, and he looks back down at the screen.

"Sorry," I say, but I'm not sure what I have to be sorry for or why I say it. I feel like I'm the one intruding or invading his space. I hover, uncertain as to whether I should carry on into the yard or turn back and put the drinks down on the kitchen table instead.

He nods his head, but his attention remains focused on his screen.

"I was, I mean, we were, Zoe and I were going to sit out here."

I can't believe how awkward I can be sometimes. He lives here as much as we do. He has every right to sit here in the garden. We don't have special privileges just because we lived here last year, and he didn't.

He waves his hand at the empty seats. There are four white metal chairs around the table, including the one on which he is sitting; there is room for all of us to sit. Now that I have almost been invited, I can do nothing other than take one of the free spaces, put the mugs down onto the table, and sit, uncomfortably, while I wait for Zoe.

I choose the seat opposite him. I might be able to sit at the table but taking one of the chairs next to him would feel even more weird.

I'm about to pick my mug up to drink, when I pause for a moment and ask, "Can I get you a coffee?" It's an icebreaker, I guess, but also common courtesy.

This time, he looks at me when I speak. It feels like he is appraising the situation, wondering whether to accept my offering. Perhaps he is shy. Perhaps he doesn't know how to mix with other people. Perhaps he just doesn't want to.

"Sure," he says. "Thanks."

He looks away after accepting, leaving me wondering whether I dare ask about milk and sugar. I also now have to shuffle back to my feet and go back into the kitchen to make his drink. Was there enough water in the kettle? I hope so.

I get up, leaving our drinks on the table. They will probably be cold by the time I get back out. I'm already starting to wish that I hadn't been so polite. It's not like he can't make his own drink. He lives here too, he's not a guest. He's never offered to make me anything since he got here. I don't think he's said more than twenty words to me. Still, I offered, and he accepted, so now I have to go back indoors to make coffee for him. It's my own fault for being so stupidly polite.

I'm in the kitchen, standing next to the kettle, waiting for it to reboil when Zoe comes down.

She looks at the single mug on the counter and reaches into the cupboard above me to pull hers out. I raise my hand to stop her.

"Yours is outside," I say, with a nod in the direction of the garden.

She looks confused for a second, before looking out, through the window, to see Carl at the table.

"Our mysterious housemate," she says. She makes a show of standing on her tiptoes to see out, and I hope that he doesn't notice. "That's for him?" she asks, pointing at the mug.

"Yep. I was being nice, and now our coffee is going cold outside, and I'm standing in here, glad that I don't have to make small talk."

"He's probably waiting for one of us to start a conversation, you know. It must be tough for him with us three."

"You go out then, and I'll bring this when I have finished."

She looks at me, as if I have set her a challenge, but then she shrugs, and goes out into the garden.

I force myself to look away from the kettle, remembering what they say about a watched pot never boiling. I want to get out there now; I don't want to leave Zoe alone. Steam starts to rise, and there's a reassuring click as the kettle turns itself off. I make the coffee quickly and almost splash the water over my hand. I curse under my breath, pour milk into the cup, and stir as I walk back outside.

I nudge the door open and see Zoe and Carl at the table. Zoe has taken the seat that I was in, so my only option now is to sit down next to him.

I hold out the cup and put on my best

smile.

"Hope this is okay," I say. I'm never usually this subservient, but I feel like I'm still in the realms of making a first impression.

He nods. "Thanks."

He puts his phone down on the table. I guess he has been looking at it the whole time that Zoe has been out here rather than chatting with her. I look over to Zoe, and she smiles back at me, not giving anything away.

"I didn't know if you wanted sugar."

"It's fine."

The three of us sit, and I wish for a moment that he would go back to doing whatever he was doing on his phone. At least I could talk to Zoe then without feeling quite so rude.

Zoe breaks the silence. "How's your course going?" she asks Carl. It's a very standard subject, it seems.

He nods slowly. "Good." He has both hands around his mug, as if keeping them warm. He raises it to his mouth and puts it down again before saying, "Thanks."

Zoe smiles. "What is it that you are

30

studying?"

He looks at her as though he is terribly bored. There's something in his face that makes me wish that we had never come to sit out here, but this is our garden too. We bought this table, and these chairs. Heck, we even bought the coffee. I did offer it to him though. Why am I so socially awkward? He doesn't look like someone I should be worried about talking too. He's quite tall, probably around the same height as Luke's six-feet, his hair is a neat sandy-brown crop, and now that I am close up, I can see that his eyes are a cool blue-grey. If I were poetic, I would say they are like a winter sky, but I'm not the kind of girl to be poetic about a man's eyes. What am I even thinking? I turn my gaze away as soon as I realise that I'm staring, but it seems it is too late. Carl lets out a momentary laugh.

"I feel outnumbered here," he says. Still, he settles back into his chair, releasing his cup from his grip and leaving it on the table. "I'm studying psychology. What about you two?"

The laugh has warmed the atmosphere a little, but I know that I'm blushing, and now I feel even more awkward.

"I'm doing my B.Ed.," Zoe says. "Teacher training."

He nods in understanding, and then turns his gaze to me, expectantly.

"Midwifery," I say. My voice is weak and wobbly. I don't know what's wrong with me.

He keeps looking at me, even after I have finished speaking. There's something in his expression that I can't put my finger on.

"You know, you can come down and sit with the three of us anytime, Carl. I would have said something before, but I haven't seen much of you," Zoe says.

"That's okay," he says. "I keep myself to myself mostly." Zoe nods and he continues. "I have a few friends at uni, but well, you know."

No. I don't know, not really, but Zoe and I both make the same "mmm" noise. That sound that means, *"yes, I understand"*.

"Or you can have dinner with us, or, well, whatever." Zoe really is trying hard to make him feel welcome. Her social skills have always been better than mine.

He nods again. "You see, you three are '*us*' and I'm not really part of that *unit*," he says. "I'm okay. Really."

I can see Zoe gulp, but if Carl notices, he doesn't acknowledge it in any way.

I still haven't spoken. I'm sitting between them, using my coffee as a reason to keep my mouth occupied.

Carl tips his mug, draining the last of his drink, and sets it back down on the table.

"I'm going out tonight, so, er, I'd better go and get ready," he says, getting to his feet. "I would ask you two, but I get the impression you don't go out much."

I don't know whether to take this as an insult or an observation. The whole interaction with him has left me feeling more confused than ever.

As he walks past us, into the kitchen, I hear another male voice from indoors. Luke is home.

I nudge Zoe's ankle with mine and make a *"what the heck was that about"* gesture. She shakes her head.

Luke steps out to join us and stands

33

waiting for one of us to say something. When neither of us does, he speaks. "You've finally had chance to talk to Andrew's replacement?"

Zoe and I look at each other and shrug.

"If you can call it that," I say.

I realise just how lucky we were to end up with a housemate like Luke last year. It already feels like having Carl around is going to be complicated. It's not Carl's fault, but I can't help but think that imaginary Andrew set the bar too high. Luke is easy going and fun to be around. Carl makes me feel awkward and uncomfortable. It's probably my social anxiety that's to blame. When things aren't quite right, it's usually my fault.

Maybe it will get better when we get to know each other. Maybe this is how it is going to be for the rest of the year.

Chapter Five

Just as our lectures this term are shifting towards the study of pathophysiology, the skills lab sessions are also preparing us to recognise and deal with the complications of pregnancy and childbirth. It's no use being able to determine that someone is suffering from eclampsia if you don't know how to care for them when they start to have a fit.

I hope that it is not a situation that I will find myself in whilst I'm on placement, but I know that one day this knowledge can help me to save a woman's life. One day it probably will.

I'm not a nurse. I have no experience of nursing outside of the elements that crossover with my midwifery skills. Sometimes I'm acutely aware of this fact. Since my first-year placement on the postnatal ward, where I learned how important basic nursing skills can be (and how much importance some midwifery mentors place upon them), I have tried to focus upon being a good nurse as well as a good midwife. I think I have changed my perception of what it means to be a nurse. I saw it as caring for ill people, and because that's not something specifically that I want to do I shied away from the idea. If anyone referred to me as a nursing student my hackles would rise and I would defensively tell them that I'm a student midwife, thank you very much. Now I recognise that nursing skills are those that we use to care for women and their families, and that those skills are essential to midwifery care.

"Don't forget," the lecturer tells us. "This year you will need to undertake your SPOKE placements. If you have forgotten what they are, refer to your PADs and make sure you start to book them in."

PADs, SPOKEs. There is so much jargon to get my head around on this course. The SPOKE refers to a "hub and spoke" system. The hub consists of the essential midwifery placements that we started last year and will continue through to the end of our third and final year. The SPOKE placements are designed to provide us with additional experience in units, wards and environments that fall outside of the usual maternity areas but can still offer a lot of scope for learning experience.

The lecturer is running through some of the suggested areas that we can attend as part of our SPOKE experience. "You might want to visit a diabetic clinic, a cancer treatment centre, accident and emergency. As long as you have thought about your learning outcomes and discussed them with your link tutor there is time for you to explore several options. I strongly recommend that you visit at least one of the gynaecology-related placements that you will see on your list."

I have the print-out in front of me. Early Pregnancy Unit. Colposcopy. Genito-urinary medicine clinic. Gynaecology ward. Gynae theatre. None of them sound particularly appealing.

"If you want to arrange a SPOKE placement in a surgical or other medical unit, as long as you can justify its value, talk to your link and we will do our best to support you."

Throughout the lab, my classmates turn to each other and start to chatter about which areas they are planning to visit. In all truthfulness I haven't given it much though yet. Mainly because I know that it is going to trigger my anxiety. Going to a new unit, where I don't fit in, caring for patients when I know very little about their conditions or how to treat them makes me feel very inadequate and incapable. I don't want to let these people down. I'm not the best person to be with them, and if I'm not actually helping them I feel like I would be little more than a voyeur.

Sophie and Simon are by my side, talking about their plans.

"I was looking after a woman with gestational diabetes on the antenatal ward," Simon is saying. "I think I want to go to the diabetic clinic so I can learn more about it. I felt like I knew nothing."

I'm not the only one then.

Sophie nods too. "I want to learn about epilepsy. We were visiting a woman at the beginning of last year who had been epileptic all her life, and it sounded pretty complicated, you know, sorting her meds out, making sure that she was safe, but that the drugs weren't going to harm the baby. I don't know anything about the actual condition. Disease. Disorder. Whatever it is.

I know nothing."

I try to think back over the year. Was there anyone with a medical condition or with a pregnancy-related disorder that I didn't know anything about? My memories swirl like a fog.

"I have no idea," I say.

I must have spoken too loudly, because the lecturer looks over at me and says, "For those of you who have *no idea* of where they are going to go, now is the time to start thinking. By the third term you will want to be focussing back on getting the competencies you need for your PADs."

Delivering 40 babies. Carrying out 100 antenatal checks, 100 postnatal checks. Other things that I can't remember without looking them up in my Practice Assessment Document. I know that the numbers are there, listed, waiting for me to carry out the tasks and have them signed off so that I can be approved as competent.

Maybe I will check what everyone else is doing and pick the best ideas from their placement options. The Early Pregnancy Unit at least sounds like it is related to midwifery.

"Your SPOKE placements are not formally assessed, but remember, whilst you are in practice, wearing your uniforms, you are representing the university, and you are expected to behave appropriately. These placements are not an excuse to slack off or avoid your regular maternity ward responsibilities. You will not be able to carry out the full range of duties on your elective placements, but you will give one hundred percent at all times. Is that clear?"

The students in the room, including myself, murmur a hushed agreement. It feels as though there must have been a past incident where someone did not do as the lecturer is suggesting.

"Make a list of the places that you want to visit and work out what you think will be most interesting and most beneficial. This is a learning opportunity. You are not likely to have the chance again, especially when you are qualified, so make the most of it."

Nursing isn't my dream, but I don't expect the placements to be a nightmare. I want to learn. I want to do everything I can to become a better midwife. I need to work out what it is that I need to focus on to achieve this. I have to use this opportunity to fill the gaps in my knowledge and experience that I will be able to use to support the women I care for throughout my career.

Right now, I have to start looking at the positives, or this year and these placements are going to be more stressful than educational. I stare at the list on the paper in front of me, and let my mind wander to the wards, units and specialist areas, willing myself to make the right choices, no matter how much my stomach churns at the thought of stepping out of my comfort zone.

Chapter Six

Over the following few days, I start to pull together some ideas for my SPOKE visits, but my regular maternity placements are the ones that I'm really looking forward to. I'm back to the postnatal ward on Monday, and Zoe and I have decided to spend Saturday having a girlie day together.

Both Zoe's Bachelor of Education course and my midwifery degree are a mix of placements and blocks of university time. When we are in uni, we see each other every day. We walk to lectures together, and for the most part we walk home together too. We have our lunch together whenever possible, and when we are at home we spend our evenings together. Through all that, I never get bored of her; if she tires of my company she has never told me. I have absolutely no doubt that she enjoys being with me as much as I do with her. We have been inseparable since we were toddlers. I don't think it will ever change. I hope that it won't. Spending so much time with me probably isn't helping her to work out how to get with Luke. We are six weeks into this academic year, and she is no closer to having told him how she feels.

Over a latte (me) and a mocha (Zoe), I broach the subject.

"So…Luke." I'm about as good as getting to the point as she is.

"So, Luke," she echoes, and takes another mouthful of coffee rather than saying anything else.

"Are you ever going to…" I make a gesture with my hand and stop halfway through, not quite sure where I am going with the sentence.

She raises her eyebrows and then laughs, sending the foam flying from the top of her mug.

"I think we have established by now that I'm never going to…" She tries to mimic whatever it was I was trying to do and waves her hands in the air in exasperation. "If he were interested, he would have done something by now."

"He probably thinks that if you were interested you would have done something," I say. The two of them dance around each other, figuratively, like two people who want to dance around each other, literally. I don't know what I can do to help them to get there.

"He told you that he isn't interested in dating," she says.

It's true. He did say that, but it was months ago. Things change.

"That was last Easter," I say. "He had just split up with a girl who messed him around and played him like a fool. It was a long time ago. I'm sure he has moved on, or at least I'm sure he's ready to move on."

She makes a tiny, delicate shrugging gesture. "I don't want to make myself look stupid, and I don't want to spoil our friendship. If I say something and he isn't interested…well, we can hardly carry on like we have been. As friends, I mean."

"But he is interested. He must be."

"You are only saying that because I'm your best friend and you love me. Not everyone loves me, you know." She leans in towards me conspiratorially, almost putting her elbow onto her plate.

In fairness most people that meet Zoe do think that she is wonderful. She's the clever, funny, beautiful one. I'm the chubby, anxious, plain one. It's fine. I know my place.

I open my mouth to speak, and she shakes her head. "And don't go saying that they love me more than they love you. Don't start putting yourself down. You always do this."

I know that Zoe can read my mind. It comes with spending so much time around each other.

I take a breath and change tack. "How about the two of you spend some time alone together. Without me around."

"At home? Where would you go? How would we…" She trails off, as though trying to think of a scenario.

"Yeah, sure. I could go out. I don't know. I'll think of something. You could make a nice dinner, get drinks, set up something on the TV to get him in the mood."

"If I put on a romantic movie he will run a mile, I'm sure," she says. "Besides, he knows I'm not into that sort of thing. Maybe I should go for a horror film instead."

I laugh. "Maybe. It doesn't have to be a romantic film, does it? You can cosy up next to him watching Cooking Queens."

"Seems more his thing," she smiles.

This is the kind of television programme that the three of us watch every night that we are together in the living room. Cooking competitions, antique hunts, teams of middle-aged men and women sorting through scrap heaps looking for treasure. We watch television shows as background noise that we don't have to think about while we laugh and chat.

I'm trying my best to help Zoe, but I am not the expert in matters of the heart. I make my best attempt at sounding authoritative and tell her, "If you do...you know...if you get some time with him, well, if it's going to happen, it will."

She nods, but she doesn't appear convinced.

"What about Carl?" she asks. She says Carl's name in a sigh, as though the word is painful to speak. He still hasn't integrated into our group, and although he keeps himself to himself for the most part, he does come and sit with us, silently and awkwardly, sometimes.

"If he chooses that night as one of

the nights he graces us with his presence then I think you're just unlucky," I say. I don't know what else I can say. Then I pause. It comes to me in a flash, and I speak without thinking it through. "I could ask him if he wants to come out with me."

"You and Carl? Spending time together? For me?" Her eyes widen and she stares at me, apparently lost for words.

It actually seems like the obvious solution, apart from the fact that I'm excruciatingly introverted, and I hate small talk. Sure, apart from that it seems like a great idea.

"I know," I say. "It's not going to be easy for me, and to be honest he probably won't even accept if I ask him to go somewhere, but I think it's the best way to give you and Luke the space you need."

She is nodding slowly, and I can feel myself starting to become restless at the thought of what I have offered to do.

"Pressure, though," she says. "Pressure. If you do this, and then I don't make a move, or if nothing happens, I'm going to feel terrible."

"No pressure," I say, but I can feel

my fingers start to tingle and the thought of drinking any more of my latte nauseates me. "What will be will be."

She takes a deep breath and lets out a low wordless sound. "Okay," she says. "Let's do this."

When we get back to Tangiers Court, Luke is in the kitchen, sitting at the table scrolling through his phone.

"Good afternoon?" he says. His eyes are scanning the shopping bags that we brought back with us. "Did you get food?"

"Yeah," Zoe says. "I'm going to make pasta tonight." We both know that Zoe's pasta is his favourite. His face lights up at the mention of it.

"Nice."

"Anything exciting happening?" I ask, nodding at the phone, and pulling up a chair next to Luke as Zoe starts to put the shopping away.

"Not really," Luke says. "Leeds lost again."

I don't particularly want to get into a conversation about football; I'm more interested in Luke's plans for the evening. I make a noise that I hope sounds like a vague show of interest.

"That's about it," he says, clicking his phone off and giving me his full attention. "How was town? Get anything good?"

"Apart from the pasta?" I say. "Not much that would interest you. We shopped, we had coffee, we came home."

"Veni, vidi, latte, eh?" He laughs out loud at his own joke, and I manage a smile.

"Something like that," I say. "What have you and Carl been up to? Planning a boys' night out?"

"He's alright, you know. He did come and have a chat with me earlier, but no. I don't think we are quite at going to the bar together stage yet."

"Maybe we should, you know, go out with him, try harder to be sociable."

Last year Luke did hit the student union with his course mates, but he has hardly gone out at all since we have been back. It's been once or twice at most, and strangely I hadn't even noticed until I thought about it just now.

He shrugs. "I've got lazy. I'm happy

49

just chilling at home with you two, watching whatever trashy television series Zoe has discovered. I don't think I'm hardcore enough for Carl."

Hardcore? Is that what he is? He does seem to go out every Friday and Saturday, but I know that there are students, even on a course as demanding as mine, that go out every night. We are students, it's part of the stereotype. Just because Zoe and I have settled down into our comfortable old-maid habits, and Luke has happily joined us, it doesn't mean that this is what everyone else should do. Carl is probably trying to socialise with people who don't curl up with hot chocolate and a blanket by nine o'clock, or don't think that a trip to Tesco at midnight for biscuits is an adventure. We are different, that's all it is.

As if summoned by the mention of his name, I can hear Carl coming down the stairs. He doesn't look dressed for a night out, but it's still early. He tends to wear jeans and t-shirts when he goes to uni and when he potters around the house; I've never seen him in the communal areas in sweatpants or pyjama bottoms. On Friday and Saturday nights he scrubs up, does something to his hair that makes it sit neatly in place rather than flop down onto his forehead like it does the rest of the week. When he goes out he wears one of a range of smart, ironed shirts. I don't think Luke knows how to operate an iron, but to be fair if I didn't need to press my uniform I probably wouldn't bother ironing either.

I've noticed a lot about him for someone that I barely speak to.

Carl nods at Luke and I as he comes into the living room and walks towards the fridge. Zoe is still putting our shopping away, and she steps awkwardly out of the way to let him in.

"Sorry," she says.

There's a very particular smile that she uses for strangers; it's an asymmetrical slant that looks like it is not quite sure of itself. That's the smile that she gives to Carl.

"No worries," he replies.

His voice is deep and firm. There's something about it that sounds more masculine than Luke's chirpy northern accent.

He reaches up towards the top of the

51

fridge, to the shelf that we allocated to him because we tend to use the others communally between the three of us. As he stretches, his t-shirt rises slightly. I catch myself looking at the firm, tanned flesh for a few moments too long, and I turn my gaze back to Luke.

"Not off with Damon and the guys tonight then?" I ask.

"Damon and the guys? Why not Florin and the guys? Raj and the guys? Something you aren't telling me, Vi?" Luke is ribbing me, I know, but that doesn't stop me from glowing bright red. "Something special about Damon is there?"

"I was just saving the time of listing them all off, but" I shrug, "apparently that didn't work."

Without looking over at Zoe I know that she is hanging on Luke's answer.

"I'm not going anywhere when there's pasta here," he says.

"There might be enough," Zoe says.

I flick a look at her, and then look towards Carl so that she follows my eyes and takes the hint. As if I should have to remind her what's riding on this.

52

I always feel like we are leaving Carl out when we start to talk like this in front of him. Apparently Zoe does too.

"Would you like to join us for dinner, Carl?" she adds.

I'm sure she is just being polite, but if he decides to stay in and have dinner with Luke and Zoe, it isn't going to be the most romantic meal.

Carl stops what he is doing in the fridge and draws back to look at her.

"Uh, thanks," he says. "I'm, uh, probably going to head out in an hour or so though."

Zoe nods.

I take a breath and try to sound natural. "Are you going to the union bar?"

"Something going on?" he says, and my heart almost stops. Am I that obvious? He carries on, "First you ask Luke, and then me. Do you need a drink or something?"

I let out a nervous laugh that I don't even have to fake, and then I add a sweet little shrug. "It's my last night before placements. I thought one of these guys might come out with me but…"

"I didn't sleep well last night," says

53

Zoe, filling in the gap, quickly and unprompted.

"And it doesn't look like I'm going to drag Luke away from dinner," I say.

Luke gives me a curious wide-eyed look, and nods slowly. Does he realise there is something going on here?

Carl pulls a bowl of leftovers from his shelf in the fridge and turns to grab a spoon from the draining board before replying.

"Sure," he says, as though he has made a considered decision. "I'm going out at eight. If you're ready by then, why not?"

Part of me is regretting this plan already. A full evening on my own with Carl, and in the union bar on a packed Saturday night at that. The things I do for Zoe. I give her a discreet wink, and I hope with all of my heart that this is the nudge that she and Luke need to finally get together.

Chapter Seven

In case I haven't made it clear, the student union bar on a Saturday night is not my favourite place to be. I keep reminding myself that I'm doing this for Zoe. I am doing this to give her some time alone with Luke, and that if the plan works out she might finally get together with him, after all this time.

Carl is dressed as he usually does on a weekend night out: smart and well groomed. He's never scruffy. Even when we are at home, I've never seen him without his hair brushed. He shaves every day, there's no sign of stubble. It's not that Luke is untidy, but I know for a fact that some weeks he wears the same t-shirt three days in a row.

I've done my best to try to look presentable. I borrowed Zoe's straighteners to get my hair under control, and I've even gone to the effort of throwing some make up onto my face. I have tried to match Carl's style, with a knee-length deep purple cotton dress and flat black Mary Jane shoes. I feel heavy and wobbly, and I throw a black cardigan over the top to cover my curves. This is far from being a date, of course, but I'm tagging along with a man I don't know very well on a night out that he didn't plan for me to be part of. I feel like I owe him something.

When we arrive at the bar I'm relieved that we manage to find a table. Apart from that positive note, the whole situation feels somewhat bizarre. Not only because I don't enjoy coming to the bar, but also due to barely knowing Carl. In the silence on our walk down here I reminded myself that he is our flatmate, and it's probably far more difficult for him to join our established group and start to get to know us that it is for us to make an effort to talk to him. We should have spoken to him more before now. I feel almost guilty about the way we have shut Carl out. Tonight could work out well for all of us.

I shuffle behind the table and fold my jacket onto the seat next to me.

"What do you drink?" he asks.

I sit open-mouthed, trying to decide

what to drink. Gin? Coke? I don't want to get drunk and let my brain make an idiot of me. It wasn't all that long ago that Zoe and Luke had to escort me out of here after I had an alcohol-induced anxiety attack.

"Sorry," I say. "I try not to drink too much. I'll have a couple though, I guess. Gin and tonic, please." I smile nervously, but he nods.

I would be better off not drinking at all, but I think I'm going to need one or two to lubricate the conversation.

"No problem," he says. "I don't drink a lot either. I just like being around people."

My smile turns into a grin. Not because I like being around people, because I really don't. I grin because it's such a relief to know he isn't expecting me to have a drinking race with him.

"Thanks, Carl."

He nods, and heads to the bar, without even asking for the money for my drink. I guess I will be getting the next round.

As he walks off, I look around the room, trying to see if there is anyone I recognise. There are groups around tables throughout the bar, all wearing similar clothes, all at similar levels of drunkenness. It seems that Carl is probably the best-dressed man in the room.

Over by the windows I can see Sophie with three other girls that I don't recognise. She doesn't see me looking over, and it would take me a while to push through the crowd to get to her. Also, I would definitely lose the table, and possibly lose my jacket, if I get up now. I raise my hand to see if a wave will catch her attention, but still she doesn't notice me.

"Hey." Carl is back before I realise it, sliding a glass towards me. He squeezes onto the bench; my coat sits between us like a bright pink barrier.

"Thanks," I say, and pick up my glass.

"Cheers," he says, clicking his bottle against the rim of my glass.

I nod and take a sip. I forget when I don't drink for a while how good a cold glass of gin and tonic can taste. I let it dance around my taste buds before I swallow.

"Too good," I smile.

"Have you never been into drinking?" Carl asks.

I shake my head. "It probably sounds terribly square, but I have never really been into going out. Zoe and I are cosy night in types. Weekends back home we would just stay home and watch TV with our parents." I shrug and take another drink. "And I'm not good with strangers. Sometimes I'm not good in crowds."

He regards me for a few moments before speaking again. "I would say that you and I are probably strangers," he says. "This is probably the longest conversation we have had, and we have lived together for over a month."

His words make me feel a weird stirring of negativity that I interpret as guilt. We should have tried harder to integrate Carl into the household, or to get out of our comfort zones like I'm now. If it weren't for Zoe wanting to be alone with Luke, we would perhaps have carried on as we were for the rest of the year. Carl would possibly have thought that we were anti-social nerds. He would possibly have been right.

"I'm sorry," I say. "I forget

sometimes what it is like. I mean what *we* are like."

"Luke probably only puts up with it because of his crush on Zoe," he says, as though it is nothing.

"What?" I stutter, almost spilling my gin, and settle my glass down gently on the table.

"She must have noticed. It was obvious to me within, like, a day." He laughs when he says it. He isn't judging or adding any negative inflection. "I thought she must have a boyfriend back home or something to not be, well, you know, with him." He drinks some more of his beer. "Or a girlfriend. Whatever."

The last words make me snort out a laugh too. "Boyfriend, definitely boyfriend," I say. And then, "But she doesn't, no. She hasn't got a boyfriend."

"Good to know," he says, but it doesn't sound as though he means it.

"Are your friends out tonight?" I ask.

I haven't seen him talking to anyone else since we arrived, but I have always assumed that when he comes here that he is with people he knows.

60

"You're changing the subject. Okay. Sure, yeah, a couple of lads from my course are over there."

He points the neck of his bottle towards the area we came through on our way in. It's an open space, with pool tables and retro arcade machines. There's a clunky old pinball machine in the corner and a small crowd are standing around it. I can't see anyone looking in our direction, so his friends could be any of the many young men.

"Right," I say. "Did you want to…I mean, do you want to go talk to them, or…?"

"Maybe later, sure. I thought it was probably time I got to know at least one of the people that I live with though."

I'm drinking too fast; I've nearly finished the gin that Carl brought over and it's starting to hit me already.

"Yeah. I didn't mean…"

I always say the wrong thing. My head feels fuzzy, and I'm not sure if it's the alcohol, the noise, or a rising tide of anxiety. He smiles though, and I relax a little.

"I know. You worry too much."

"Actually, I really do. I have quite severe anxiety." I might as well tell him now. If I do end up having a meltdown at least he will have been forewarned.

An expression crosses his face that I can't quite put my finger on. It's not concern, and I'm sure it's not derision. Somehow it's not sympathy either. It makes me uneasy.

"What's that like?" he asks.

I find the question as strange as his expression. It's not something that relative strangers usually ask.

"What's it like?" I repeat. "I'm better than I was."

"What's it like though? What happens?" He sits back, as if settling to hear a story from me.

"Like an anxiety attack," I say.

"I don't know anything about anxiety. Tell me what happens."

I pause, take a mouthful of my drink, and realise that I have drained the glass. I look at him for a few moments before I reply.

"It's not always the same. Sometimes it's just this inexplicable abject fear of…" I pause again, trying to get this right. "Fear of failure. Fear of the future. Fear that everything I do is going to be, I don't know, wrong, I suppose, but worse than that. It's the fear that I will just mess up everything I try to do. That's what happens in my head anyway. Sometimes it's what happens in my body that hits me the hardest though. I get dizzy, like I can't focus on anything. My heart feels like it's going to explode; it's all over the place, fast and thudding. I can't breathe properly. I feel sick, my stomach…it's like being drunk sometimes."

I stop to take a breath. I can feel my heart pounding now, even talking about my anxiety makes me anxious.

Carl is looking at me with an emotionless expression. His composure feels out of place considering what I have told him. There's something else though. There's still something else. That's what's unsettling me. There's something else, and I don't know what it is.

I expect him to say something, but for ten, maybe fifteen, seconds he says nothing. We sit in silence looking at each

63

other. I've probably freaked him out. I thought that being open was a good plan, but now it seems that I was completely wrong.

Finally, he says, "Another drink?"

I squint in surprise and look down at my glass, even though I know it is empty.

"It's my round," I say. My voice sounds like sandpaper.

"I'll get them, it's fine."

"Okay," I rasp. "Coke then, please."

He gets up without saying anything else and goes over to queue for the bar.

I wish we were sitting near the window; I need some air. Perhaps I wish that I were sitting near the window so that I could be with Sophie and her friends instead of here with Carl. Tonight is turning out to be a terrible idea.

The thought of 'tonight' reminds me of why I'm actually here. Zoe. I pull out my phone and check for messages. There's one.

How's it going with Carl? I owe you one. xx

I'd say that she owes me more than one. This is painful. I guess that I'm finding out why Carl doesn't mix with us at home.

I message Zoe back.

Terrible. Anything happening there? xx

I send the text and pause, wondering for a second whether I should pop a message to Sophie, and tell her that I'm here. She might come over and invite me to join them. What am I thinking? Carl has left *his* friends to sit here with me, I can't up and leave now.

Before Zoe has the chance to reply to the text, Carl is back.

"Everything okay?" He nods towards my phone.

Should I be honest? Probably.

"I was checking in with Zoe," I say.

"She wanted to know if I was behaving like a gentleman?" he asks.

I cough slightly in surprise. "No! I mean, I was checking what she was doing. I thought that Luke…well, we thought that if she had some time alone with Luke she might, they might…" I'm stumbling over my sentences, and I know I must sound like a clumsy idiot. It makes me feel more anxious, and I don't think I should say anything else. My brain is a mushy jumble of words. I hate this.

"You only came out with me so that they could do whatever it is that they have spent the last year not doing?" He looks offended and I get a heavy feeling in my gut as though I have swallowed a bowling ball.

"No," I say, speaking slowly and carefully. But it is the truth, isn't it? That *is* why I'm here. "Sort of." There's another awful silence before I continue. "Not just that. I want to get to know you. I do. It's silly that we live in the same house and hardly speak. It's like, you know, killing two birds with one stone." It's a bad metaphor for this situation. "Sorry," I say. "I'm sorry."

He shakes his head, but he doesn't stand up and leave. "It's hard being the new guy when everyone knows each other. I'm…" He pauses, as though it's his turn to think of the right words to say. "I'm not as confident as you might think I am."

It strikes me as a strange thing to say. I don't have any preconceived ideas about his confidence or lack of confidence. It has never crossed my mind.

"I find it difficult to talk to people," he says. "And with you and Zoe and Luke already so close and so happy, well, I suppose I didn't think that there was room for me."

He reaches his hand out across the table and places it on top of mine.

"I'm so touched that you could open up to me," he says. "It must be difficult to talk to someone you don't know very well about your anxiety. I'm sorry that I flipped out a bit there about you only coming out with me to help Zoe."

"You…you didn't flip out. Not really." I look at his hand, but I don't pull back. "It's fine."

"Thank you," he says in a calm, measured tone. "Thanks Violet. Now, shall we start again?"

Although I'm slightly puzzled, I smile, happy to be back on track towards at least a half-decent evening.

"That would be lovely," I say.

When he smiles back, I catch myself for a split-second thinking that the man sitting next to me, with his hand on mine, is actually quite attractive. Perhaps it's the gin. I haven't had this kind of thought about Carl before, but when have I taken the time to stop to look at him, or to even speak with him properly? I hope I'm not blushing, but I fear that my cheeks are starting to fill.

I'm here for Zoe. I definitely don't need to start thinking about anything else. I shake the thoughts out of my head and resolve not to drink any more alcohol tonight. I don't want to end up making a fool of myself in any one of the number of ways that I potentially could. No more alcohol, and no more thoughts about blue eyes and how I have been single for far too long.

Chapter Eight

By the time we get back to Tangiers Court it's almost midnight. I feel a little woozy, but I'm not what I would classify as 'drunk'. Tipsy maybe, but that's all I'll admit to. Carl was actually very understanding about me not wanting to drink much, especially after I'd told him about the anxiety, and the way that alcohol can affect me. It ended up being a decent evening, all things considered.

I haven't heard from Zoe for the last couple of hours. I want to assume that it's a good sign, that she was too busy with Luke to message me. When I walk past the living room though I see her on the sofa, tucked under Luke's cosy fleece blanket, curled asleep. He's in the armchair and he puts his finger to his lips as I look in, as if I can't see that Zoe is sleeping.

I turn to Carl and pass on the finger on the lips gesture. He nods in acknowledgement, and then points to the kitchen. As quietly as possible, we pick our way down the hall, and slouch down at the table. Luke is only a few paces behind us.

He closes the kitchen door softly, so as not to wake Zoe, and asks, "Coffee?"

"Sure, thanks," Carl says, and I nod my head too.

It feels strange, the two of them here with me and Zoe not with us. It's like there's an imbalance in the room. It also feels strange that I have no idea what has happened with Zoe and Luke tonight, and the one person that I want to ask about it is fast asleep. I know I can't say anything to Luke, not without speaking to Zoe first, but I'm itching to find out.

The whole room is shimmering, a haze of mild intoxication, when suddenly it hits me that I didn't tell Carl not to say anything about Zoe's feelings. I really shouldn't have mentioned it to him. I can't believe what a big, stupid mouth I have. I'm starting to panic; I can feel my forehead heating up and a clammy dampness rising through my skin.

"You okay, Violet?" Carl asks. He leans over the table to me and puts his hand flat against my skin. "You're burning up." He gets up and opens the back door, letting in the cool autumnal night. It feels fresh and welcome, but it doesn't make me feel any better.

"Uh, I might sit outside," I say, pushing myself up from the table and wobbling to my feet.

"Careful," he says. "Maybe you had a couple too many. We were pretty restrained though." He smiles, and it's such a gentle, caring smile. It does nothing to help me to cool down.

Carl gets up too and puts his hand on my arm to steady me.

"I can bring the drinks out," Luke says. He is still keeping his voice as quiet as possible, ever conscious of the sleeping Zoe in the other room.

I'm about to say that it's okay, and that I will be fine here, but Carl speaks first.

"Thanks, mate," he says. "I'll come out with you, Vi. I could do with some air too."

I pass a quick look to Luke and he raises his eyebrows, but only says, "Sure, fine."

In the garden, we sit at the pretty metal table. Fairy lights glow around the trellises like fireflies. The night is clear and quiet, and not as cold as it should be for November.

"Are you sure you're okay?" Carl asks.

I look over his shoulder and through the window into the kitchen, where Luke is pouring hot water into our mugs. "Yeah," I say. I lean towards him so that I can speak more quietly and still be heard. "I was worrying, panicking I suppose. I should have told you earlier, you know, not to say anything to Luke about how Zoe feels."

He smiles, but there's something cold about the expression, as though the smile is concealing his true feelings.

"Okay," he says.

"Okay?" I echo. His response is not helpful.

"Okay," he says again, flatly.

I look at him in a way that I hope conveys my confusion.

"Okay, really. Look, they obviously both feel it, if they are too dumb to get it together, well it's definitely not my problem."

"They aren't dumb," I say,

defensively. "Zoe is my best friend. She isn't dumb. And neither is Luke. They are just -"

"What? What are they?" Before I can say anything else, Luke comes into the garden, and I'm forced to stop talking.

"Any better, Violet?" he says.

"Uh, yeah. Thanks. I was…I needed some air. Thanks."

"Did you have a good night?" Carl asks.

"We watched TV; Zoe fell asleep. The usual exciting Saturday night in Tangiers Court," Luke smiles. I watch his face, trying to work out if there was anything else that he doesn't want to talk about here, in front of Carl. He doesn't give me any sign. "What about you two? How was the union?"

Carl shrugs. "Same as ever."

"I know what you mean," Luke says.

If nothing else comes of tonight, I think it's a good thing that Carl is finally talking to us, or should that be that we are finally talking to him? Luke is chatting to him now as though he is a friend, rather than someone who has lived with us all this time and never bothered to have a conversation. I shake the thought away, reminding myself that it was down to us as much as Carl, if not more so. Tonight, at the bar, it was fine. For Saturday night in the union bar to be anything other than an ordeal is a plus for me. We chatted, we laughed, and now, here we are, sitting together in our garden, feeling like friends.

"I quite liked it," I say, although my thoughts are distant. It could be the drink, or perhaps the ambience, but I feel strangely peaceful. I'm drifting. I could probably close my eyes and -

"Oh, and I kissed Zoe," Luke says.

I snap back from my reverie.

"Nice," Carl says. "About time."

I want to shake him, ask what he's doing reacting like that, making it obvious that he knew what was going on, but Luke laughs, and Carl joins in. Of course, it was clear to Carl, before I even told him, he knew there was something going on. Or at least that something should have been going on.

"About time," I repeat, and I smile at Luke.

"I'm not going to kiss and tell, so don't go asking me for details," he says. "Besides, I wouldn't want to deprive Zoe of the chance to gossip all about it."

I reach over and put my hand onto his arm. "I'm so pleased," I say. "I can't believe it took you both this long, but…yes, I'm so pleased that you're finally getting it together."

Luke looks at me, and I pause. A feeling of panic runs through me like electricity.

"You are, aren't you? Getting it together? It wasn't…I mean, it…you…?"

From the doorway comes a familiar voice, sounding happier than I have heard it in a long time.

"We are," Zoe says. "We are definitely, finally getting it together."

My body seems to have forgotten that a couple of minutes ago I was ready to drift off into a peaceful doze. I leap to my feet and rush over to her.

"Zoe!" I scoop her up into a hug, my arms wrapping all the way around her petite frame, lifting her slightly off the floor in my excitement.

She makes a happy squeaking noise, and under any other circumstances, with any other man, I would probably shush her, tell her to play it cool, and not look so excited in front of him, but this is Luke. This is different. This is perfect.

Chapter Nine

I stay up way too late, talking to Zoe about what happened, or more precisely, how it happened. The bottom line is that she finally told Luke how she feels, and he said something like she shouldn't have waited so long to tell him, and boom, they kissed. I'm sure it was all very romantic and sweet. I'm happy for her, but I don't know if I will ever experience anything similar. I worry too much, I panic, I stress, I overreact, I'm over-protective of my own feelings. Zoe throws herself in, albeit after waiting around for months this time, but still, when she does it, she gives one hundred percent. I wish I could be like her. If I were as pretty, as smart, as likeable as she is, perhaps I could be. If I were less anxious, perhaps, perhaps.

This week I will be back on placement, which feels like perfect timing. I'm not around the house so much, as the shift pattern is a mixture of early mornings and late evenings. I won't be getting in their way. I try to shake that feeling out of my head as soon as I think it, but wasn't my presence what kept the two of them apart for so long? It took me going out with Carl to encourage them to finally make a move. I want Zoe to be happy, but what if she can't be while I'm around? My shifts will give them space, and I hope that's enough.

Being back on the postnatal ward means working with Geri Smith again. Last year I almost gave up on my placement with her after the first day. She is strict, demanding and doesn't accept anything other than one hundred percent effort. She was exactly what I needed. She pushed me to learn, to increase my practical knowledge, and my nursing skills. I can't wait to see her.

When I turn up to the ward on Monday afternoon, there is a girl sitting in the office, wearing the same student midwife uniform as I am. I don't recognise her, so she's either a first year or final year student. From her timid expression I assume it's the former.

"Hi," I say, with a big smile. "I'm Violet."

"Shell," she says. She manages to smile back, just about.

"Are you alright?" I ask. "Are you on the morning shift?"

She shakes her head roughly. "Community," she says. So, she is a first year. "My mentor is picking up some paperwork and she wanted to visit one of the ladies."

"You didn't want to go with her?" I ask, confused.

"I don't know her. The patient, I mean. It's my first day out. I haven't met her, so…"

I nod. "You can still go with your mentor though. What's her name?"

"The woman?"

"Your mentor."

"Oh. Of course." She blushes, and answers, "Sarah Godley."

She's in the same team as the community midwife I had my placement with this time last year. Did I look like this twelve months ago? Shell is like a rabbit in the headlights, wide-eyed and nervy.

"You'll have a great time. Look, can I get you some tea, or…"

I'm cut off by Geri coming through the doors, calling my name.

"Violet Cobham! My favourite student has returned!" Geri says. Favourite? Well, that is a surprise to me. Either that, or she says the same thing to everyone.

The timid girl curls even more tightly inside her shell. Shell. Her name seems appropriate.

"Hi Geri," I enthuse, and stand up to give her a gentle hug. "I'm happy to be back."

"Are you here too?" Geri barks the words at Shell. The poor girl looks like she is on the edge of tears.

I shake my head and answer for her, without thinking. "She's on community. Waiting for Sarah Godley."

"Make the tea, do something useful," Geri says to the girl. She brushes her hand in the air as though she is trying to waft away a fly.

"I was just about to get it," I say, "but I'll show Shell the kitchen."

"Good girl," Geri says with a big smile. She doesn't mean it to sound condescending, I know, having been here with her last year, but I'm sure that Shell is not getting the best first impression of my

80

mentor.

When we get into the kitchen, Shell speaks. "Who is that? I'm glad she's not my mentor."

"She's fine," I say. I try to keep my voice pleasantly chirpy and stop myself from sounding defensive. I remember how I felt last year when I started on my community placement, and again when I first met Geri. "Honestly," I smile at her. "All of the midwives here are lovely. Don't worry."

Don't worry. I've dealt with anxiety and panic attacks since I was eleven and here I am telling someone else not to worry. Seeing this girl reminds me of who I was last year. I have achieved so much since then, academically and personally.

The girl nods, but stands rigid, her hands grasped in front of her, one inside the other, in a stiff, tight pose.

I fill the huge heavy teapot with boiling water and stack the mugs next to the milk and sugar on the tray. I have done this so many times before, and doing it again today feels like a kind of homecoming. I was on this ward for six weeks last spring, and I never realised how much I missed it until now.

"Do you always have to make the tea?" Shell asks.

"I always offer," I say. "Unless someone beats me to it." I give her another smile. She's going to think smiling is all I ever do.

Shell says nothing, but I feel her silent judgement. I don't care. She will learn what I have learned: being part of the team is more than fulfilling my midwifery duties.

I pick up the tray and gesture for her to follow me back into the office. The other staff members have started to arrive for the shift by the time I place it down onto the heavy wooden desk.

"Violet!"

"You're back!"

"Nice to have you with us."

Voices come at me from all around the room, and my smiles turn into a grin.

Shell stands by the door, watching as I lift the pot and pour hot tea into the mismatching mugs.

"Want one?" I offer.

Shell turns to look down the corridor, I expect she is trying to see whether Sarah is finally on her way. She looks back at me, nervously.

"I'm sure it's fine," I tell her.

If Sarah is anything like Stacey, the mentor that I had in community last year, no doubt she will have a lot to talk about with the woman she has gone to visit. When you have got to know someone like that I'm sure there's plenty to say. I haven't had the opportunity to see someone through from antenatal to postnatal yet, but I hope that I'll have the chance soon.

I thrust a mug towards Shell, and then take my place amongst the postnatal ward staff for the afternoon shift. It's not a big office, and we are all crammed in, squashed onto desk chairs, low armchairs, and perched on tables. There's no room for Shell to sit, so she hovers in the doorway, clutching her drink and listening in.

I feel at home here now. Everything seems to be falling into place. I'm so much more at peace this year. Apart from the few occasional blips, I have rarely had the slightest glimmer of anxiety. When I have, it has passed quickly. I have dealt with it.

I feel like everything I'm learning as a student midwife is also helping me to grow as a person. I'm learning to help others, but in doing so, I'm helping myself. This time last year, I was the meek, timid girl that Shell is now. I was worse than that. I fled from my first practical exam because I couldn't even handle thinking about it when I was in the skills lab. I panicked about my placements; I was a mess. Now, I'm calmly making tea for all the midwives, trying to reassure this student, and feeling nothing but excitement and confidence for my placement.

Just before handover starts, Shell's mentor returns, and pops her head into the office.

"Hi everyone," Sarah says. She turns to Shell and asks, "Ready to go?"

Shell looks at her almost full mug of tea, and then back at her mentor.

"Yes, sure." Her eyes scan the room looking for somewhere to put her drink down.

"The tea is hot if you want one before you go," I offer. Last year I wouldn't have spoken to any midwife that I didn't know. Last year, I would have been the girl looking for somewhere to put her mug and run along with my mentor.

"Great," Sarah smiles. "Finish yours too," she says to Shell.

The corners of Shell's mouth turn up, and she raises the tea to her lips. I know that she is going to be fine. I hope that by this time next year she is offering kindness and tea to another new student. I wonder where I will be then.

Chapter Ten

I'm on an early shift on Tuesday, and Zoe is on her placement at the school. We have agreed to meet up at Blackheath's cafe in the town centre after we finish, for a catch up.

Yes, we live together, and we can catch up any time that we want to, but sometimes it's good to have some dedicated girl time. No interruptions, just me and my best friend. Besides, Blackheath's has the best Bakewell slices in Wessex.

I've already drunk my latte, and my cake is only crumbs on my plate when I steel myself to bring up something that has been on my mind. Zoe and I have never shied from discussing personal issues, but now that her boyfriend is someone that we live with, somehow things feel different.

"You and Luke...well, you don't seem to be all that physical with each other. Not around me, anyway."

I feel awkward saying it, and I can't hold eye contact with her. It's not so much that I'm worried about how their budding relationship is progressing, I'm worried that

I'm getting in the way.

She makes a tiny laughing noise, that sounds more like surprise than amusement.

"Well, what do you want us to be like? Would you rather that we were all over each other?" she says. I can't read her voice, even though I know her better than anyone else. I can't tell what she is thinking, not now.

I'm looking at my plate, pushing the last flake of almond around with the tip of my fork.

"No." I look up. "No. I mean, it's just, I don't know. I don't want you to have to rein it in or hold back just because I'm always around." I want to say, 'in the way', but as I think the words I realise how self-pitying they would sound, so I cut the sentence off.

She bats the words away. "Don't be silly. I want you around. I want you around, always. I do."

"He might not feel the same," I say. "Have you even talked about it?"

She pauses just long enough for me to realise that they must have indeed discussed it.

"You have?" I say. "And, what? What did he say?" Now I'm not looking away from her; now she has my full attention. I have to know what's been said. I start to feel that familiar rush of nausea as my anxiety floods my body.

"Hey, relax," she says, reading me better than I read her. "Nothing bad. Do you really think I would ever say anything bad about you?"

"Not you," I mutter, and this time I can't hold the pathetic words back.

"Luke?" She sounds incredulous. "You think that he would?"

I roll my eyes, at my own stupid thoughts more than anything else. Then I silently shake my head.

"Violet. I don't want things to be any different than they are. I don't know, maybe subconsciously this is why I didn't approach Luke for all that time. Maybe it's what stopped him too."

"Me? You both blame me for being in the way?"

"Violet!" She snaps my name this time, and then reaches out her hand, placing it on my arm when I look away. "I'm sorry.

I didn't mean to be so sharp. What you're saying though, it doesn't make sense. I have never treated you like you're in the way, and I never will. Do you really think that?"

I sigh. "I'm just worried that you can't be natural with him, that you can't have the kind of relationship that you would if I weren't around."

"I wouldn't even be living here with him if you weren't around. That is what makes it weird for me, that I live with him. I always thought that I would meet someone, date for a while, six months, a year, more, and then maybe choose out somewhere to live together."

"We used to look at that block of apartments by the pier. You wanted to live there."

"And you were going to move into the flat next door to me. I remember."

We always shared our dreams, our hopes for the future. Being here at university is one of the goals that we have actually achieved. I don't know if I ever believed that training to be a midwife, living with Zoe, would actually happen. Sometimes when I picture something that I really want to do my brain tells me that I will never really do it, that I'm stupid for wanting things that I will never have. Did I really ever think that Zoe and I would live next door to each other in beachfront apartments in the town we grew up in? A part of me must have believed in it.

She gives me the tender, soft smile that makes me feel warm and safe.

"Instead we have moved into a cosy student house, and I met the man of my dreams. Sometimes things just happen, don't they? I wouldn't have planned it this way, but I'm happy with how things are. I want you to be happy too, Violet."

Happy. It's an interesting word. I am content. I have every reason to be happy. I made it here. I'm getting through my course. I've met some great people in my classes, but I haven't really made friends. I adore my placements; being in my uniform, on the wards makes me feel something that I don't get from anything else. I love the little house that we have made a home. I get to see my best friend every day. But something is missing. I don't know what it is. Perhaps it is the way that anxiety taints everything I do. I can never actually relax and enjoy things, because at the back of my mind - and sometimes at the front of my mind - I feel like everything is going to fall apart.

"For the record," she says, "Luke was concerned about you. He said that he didn't want to make you feel uncomfortable or awkward."

"He's a good one," I smile. "He wasn't just saying that to make you happy, was he?" There I go again. I can't just accept things the way they are. I have to think about the negative side.

Zoe laughs, and I assume that she thinks I'm joking. Good. It's better that way. Better for her.

"You two should do some normal things. You know, go out for a walk to the beach together, take him to see a movie, I don't know, have dinner out or drinks, or -"

"Go on a date," she says.

"Yeah," I say. They seem to have skipped that part of the relationship and gone from just housemates to housemates-that-are-in-a-relationship without doing any of the fun things that people do at the start of a relationship. Not that I know much about it, but those are the things that I like. That 'getting to know each other' phase is my favourite. The thrill of the new. I don't much like the chase, that part where you are trying to work out whether someone likes you or not, but when you both work out where you stand, and start talking, exploring each other, that's the fun part.

Zoe is quiet for a few seconds while she thinks this over. It's as though I have suggested something ground-breaking, but it seems pretty obvious to me.

"It would do you good to have some time out alone together. You can make out all you like, and not have to worry about making me blush."

This raises another laugh from Zoe. "I'm not sure that we are likely to snog each other's faces off in public, to be honest, but it would be nice to have a date. What about you though, what would you do?"

"Do?" I ask. "I could come along to carry your bag for you, I suppose."

She bats me with her hand. "Silly. I mean -"

"I know what you mean. You have to stop thinking like that. You aren't responsible for me. I can fill my time on my own, you know." I smile, but actually I don't feel completely confident that what I'm saying is true. I have never really spent much time in my own company. Not that I have had many relationships, but I have always had Zoe. Even when the two of us have dated people in the past, we have always had time together too.

"I'll ask Carl to babysit you," she smiles.

Perhaps I would spend more time talking to Carl if Luke and Zoe weren't around. I don't ever want to live in a world without Zoe, but I wonder how different things would be if she weren't here. If I had to do everything alone, would I even have got to university? I doubt it.

I don't respond to her joke. Instead I ask, "So, where will you go?"

She grins, and the two of us tumble into her bubble of happiness, thinking up ideas and making plans.

Chapter Eleven

Luke loves Zoe's idea of date night, and dutifully starts to make arrangements. They go out for pizza for their first proper date, and I'm sadder about missing out on the food than I am about missing Zoe's company for the evening.

On their second date night I don't have any plans of my own, and I'm on my own in the living room. I could have thought of something to do; I could have gone out with Sophie, Ashley and Simon, or any combination of the group, but instead I decided to stay in and enjoy my alone time. Alone, that is, until Carl comes into the living room.

"Do you mind if I join you?"

The noise startles me, and I can feel my heart thundering. It doesn't take much to tip me onto the brink of a panic attack sometimes. I'm flimsy, I know.

"Uh, yeah, I mean, no, sure, come in." I try to gather my words, so I don't sound like a gibbering idiot.

Carl is dressed in a pair of black

jeans and a white t-shirt with a faded print. His feet are bare, I notice as he flops into the chair and stretches his legs out in front of him.

"What are we watching?" he asks.

My mind goes blank for a moment. To be honest, I have been scrolling through my phone, and the Netflix show on the television really is just background noise.

"You can change it if you like." I toss the control into his lap.

"Okay," he says, and starts to read through the menu.

I suppose it's only polite that I put my phone down now, so I do. I feel a little disgruntled that I have been interrupted from my nothingness, but I remind myself that Carl lives here too and has just as much right to sit here and watch trashy television as I do.

"Salvage Den alright for you?"

It's the kind of programme that Zoe and I would choose.

"Sure. Anything."

He switches it on, and we both sit in awkward silence through the first five minutes.

I can't bear it much longer.

"Can I get you a drink? Tea, coffee? Beer?" I don't even know what he drinks.

"Fetch me a beer back, thanks," he says. I suppose he assumes that I was going anyway. I am now.

When I come back with the drinks he shows me a big smile. It seems a little forced, but maybe he is just trying to be friendly.

"Thanks so much, Violet," he says.

"No problem," I reply, and take my seat back on the sofa, with my brew.

Somehow I feel more comfortable with a prop. I can sit and drink my coffee and not feel like I should be chatting to Carl. Apparently, now that he has a beer, he thinks just the opposite.

"Zoe and Luke out tonight?" he asks.

"Um, yeah." It's fairly obvious, so he must just be making conversation.

"Anywhere nice?"

"Dinner, I think. I mean they weren't here for dinner, so, you know."

He nods and falls silent again for a short time.

He speaks again. "I feel a bit of a

gooseberry down here with those two around, you know. I don't mean to be anti-social, I just, I don't know. I feel like I am in their way sometimes."

"I'm sure they don't mean to make you feel like that." I immediately jump to Zoe's defence, even though I can totally understand how he feels.

"I know. I don't think they do it on purpose." He laughs, as though I have made a joke rather than said something stupid. "I'd rather give them the space."

"It's your home too," I say.

"And yours," he nods.

"Yeah, I mean, it's not all about them. If you want to come in here and spend time, there's room for you. I mean, you are always welcome. No one thinks you're a gooseberry."

"I think I am. Do you never feel like that?"

I look at him. Do I admit to it, and possibly reflect badly on Zoe, or should I cover up my feelings?

"I think it's good for them to have some time alone together away from here," I deflect.

He laughs again. "You're very loyal to your friend. I like it. I respect that."

He has a deep, earthy voice, and his laughter is like soft shale. I find myself wanting to hear more.

"But you do know what I'm talking about," he says. It's not a question, this time. I don't give him an answer. Instead I shuffle in my chair and focus on the television.

Unfettered, he carries on with the questions. It's not like I'm engrossed in the show, but I'm not used to being interrogated. At least it's not small talk. It feels as though the questions he is throwing at me run far deeper than that.

"Do you not go out much?" he asks.

He's lived here with us for nearly three months; I'm sure he already knows the answer to the question.

"I'm more a bath and book type," I smile. I know I must sound terribly boring to him. He is probably used to far more interesting conversations with far more interesting people. "We do go out shopping at the weekend though. There's a great cafe in town and -" I know this wasn't the type of going out that he meant, so I shut my mouth.

He looks at me as though prompting me to say more. "Well, you don't need to hear about it," I say, quietly.

"I'm trying to get to know you," he says. His voice is soft and gentle now, as though I'm a wild animal he is trying to approach and calm. I'm more like a pet hamster than a feral cat though.

"I know, I'm sorry. I'm not used to anyone wanting to get to know me," I say, and immediately wish I hadn't. I must sound stupid.

"I'm sure that's not true," he says with a kind, warm smile.

"Tell me about yourself. I hardly know anything about you." I ask, trying to deflect the attention onto him.

He shrugs and puts his beer bottle to his mouth, knocking back a deep gulp.

"Not much to tell. I come from Leicester, I'm studying psychology, I like football and going out with the lads. I don't think there's anything exceptional about me."

"Why did you choose Wessex University?"

He pauses before answering, and I

see something cross over his face that I think could possibly be sadness. It's hard to tell, but his expression changes, briefly.

"I wanted to get as far away from home as I could," he says. "London was too expensive. Wessex is near the sea, and near the countryside, and I was told there was meant to be a good social scene. What's not to like."

I grew up half an hour away from here. I suppose I take for granted the things that people like about the area. Tourists flock here for the beach and the beauty spots, but I don't think I have even bothered to go down to the promenade in the past year. I could say that I don't have time, but I can make time. It's not like I have a hectic social life.

"Fair enough," I say. "Zoe and I come from Portland. It's half an hour down the coast."

"I thought you two must have been friends for longer than a year. You're too close to only have met as Freshers."

I nod. "I've known her all my life."

"That's why you're so defensive then," he says, more to himself than to me, "and so caught up in each other."

"Caught up?" I can't tell whether he means it as an insult or merely an observation.

"You follow each other around, always in each other's pockets. I've lived here for three months, and this is the first time that I have ever had chance to talk to you alone."

My eyes can't meet his. I know that it is true, but I have never wanted it any other way.

"It's fine," he says. "If you're happy, it's fine. I have been wondering though…" He stops mid-sentence.

"What?" I ask. He knows how to get my attention, that's for sure.

"Wondering whether it's good for you. You're kind of living in her shadow. It would be good for you to have your own friends, do your own thing." He stops, shakes his head, and drains the rest of the bottle of beer. "I've said too much."

Maybe he has. I'm not sure.

"I have friends," I say. "I know people on my course."

"Course mates. That doesn't really

count. What about at home? Before you came here?"

I shake my head. "We know a few other people, sure."

"We," he echoes. "What about you?"

It's starting to feel very hot in here. The room is large enough for a sofa, two armchairs and the unit that houses our television, but right now it feels tiny. I'm getting claustrophobic in my own home. This is not good.

Suddenly, it's like there's a shift in energy in the room, like a switch has been flicked.

"I didn't mean to make you feel bad," Carl says. His voice is soft and sweet like honey. "You seem like an interesting person. I barely know you. I shouldn't make assumptions."

He's right. He's right about me being an extension of Zoe, or that we are extensions of each other. She is all I have ever known. Being her friend is all I have ever been. I have never questioned it, but now, with Luke taking up so much of her time, where does that leave me. Who am I without her?

I shake my head slowly. My face is burning, and I can feel tears prickling my eyes. I wipe my face, trying to look casual, and hoping that he doesn't catch on to my emotions.

"It's fine. Really. I appreciate your honesty." And I do. It's uncomfortable but refreshing. Carl says what he thinks, he just comes out with it, and what he has told me is true. "You're right," I say. "I have probably been too dependent on her."

It's a criticism of myself, not Zoe. She's not the one to blame.

Carl nods, and again he gives me that smile. It's friendly, reassuring and kind. Despite his words making me question so much about my life, I somehow feel safe here with him now. Those anxious uprisings are settling within me.

Chapter Twelve

Shift work means early mornings, late nights, and sometimes overnight sessions at the hospital. The mornings start at half past seven, the afternoons finish at ten at night. Some staff work a full day which is, appropriately, called a "Long Day". Even though choosing Long Days means only having to work three days out of the week, I don't think I have the stamina to give my complete focus and attention for that long in one chunk. Geri works a regular five-day-week, so I follow her shift pattern. All of the midwives have their working days scheduled onto a planner referred to as the "off-duty", although it effectively tells you when you are *on* duty.

Looking on the bright side, after working Monday late and Tuesday morning I have Wednesday off before two afternoon shifts; then I'm on the rota for Saturday morning. As a qualified midwife I would be paid a little extra for the weekend shift; as a student, I do it because I need to experience what it is like to work the shift pattern. It's also useful to learn what happens differently on different days.

During the week, there are elective inductions, where women come to the antenatal ward (or sometimes to the delivery suite directly) to have their labours started artificially. They are usually past their due dates, but there are other reasons for induction too.

There's a theatre list most weekdays, for women who need to be booked for elective caesarean sections. Elective makes it sound like they *want* to have the surgery, which isn't always the most accurate way to describe them. Planned caesareans captures it more precisely. Women who need to have caesareans for clinical reasons are booked onto the surgery list, and as there are more doctors available Monday to Friday, that's when the list runs.

There are, of course, women who were planning to give birth the 'normal' way and experience complications that mean they need to have caesareans - and that can happen any day, at any time. Also, women who have been planning caesareans can go into labour. Sometimes they can deliver vaginally, but sometimes they still need to have the caesarean they were booked in for, just ahead of schedule. What all of this means is that whilst some things are planned, and some things are expected, when it comes to the human body, you never really know what is going to happen.

On Friday, the domestic assistant has wheeled the dinner trolley around the ward, and I have just returned to the office after helping her to dish out the evening meal.

"There's a section coming up from Delivery," Geri says. She still slips into this habit of referring to women as 'a section', 'a delivery', 'a multip'. I'm not a fan. Reducing the person to their experience or their condition is rooted in the medical tradition that Geri, many of the other nurses, and all of the doctors have been trained in. I like to believe that I will never feel that way and will never treat anyone as a patient rather than a person. It's easy to use the word "patient" as shorthand, but they are women, first and foremost.

I nod at Geri and wait for her to give me further details. She's in the middle of eating a cup of soup, dipping thick white bread into the red tomato, like a swab into blood. My mind makes too many connections like that when I have been out on the ward for a few days. Strangely, it doesn't turn my stomach; it has become sort of normal.

"Fay Curtis. Uh, failed forceps."

An emergency caesarean then. She will have been in labour and got so far into her delivery that she was on the point of pushing the baby out, and something went wrong. I will read her notes when she comes up, but a caesarean for failed forceps usually means that the baby has been distressed, the heartbeat dropping, the blood becoming acidic. If the mother's cervix is fully dilated and the baby is low enough down the birth canal, sometimes it is possible to use forceps to help baby to be born. If that fails, it's straight into the theatre so the baby can be delivered quickly.

"It's her first baby. She wants to breastfeed." Geri dips her bread again, and a large splash drips back into the cup before she lifts it up to her mouth.

"Okay," I say. "How long?"

"They're just cleaning her up, and then bringing her."

I nod. "I'll get a space ready."

From theatre, women are usually transferred into a small recovery room for post-operative observations, and after half an hour, or sometimes a little longer if necessary, they are transferred up to postnatal. Regardless of whether they have had a general anaesthetic or a spinal (where they are given a local anaesthetic into the space around the bones in the spine), they aren't able to walk, so they are brought up on a bed, and we wheel one of ours out in a straight swap. I'll move the bed out of one of our bays, and the recovery midwife and theatre assistant will bring the bed with Fay on it to fill the space. Where possible, we try to allocate the post-operative ladies to side rooms, so I write Fay's name on the board in one of the appropriate spaces.

The postnatal ward runs on a pattern of routine. We have our handover at the beginning of shift, then it's the drug round before we visit every patient to check that she and her baby are fit and well. The assistants go around with refreshments, and the catering staff take the meals. For those women who are post-op, the loop of routine is doubled up with more frequent observation, and usually additional drugs.

There are checklists to cover every eventuality: daily observations for mother and baby, drugs charts, fluid balance, discharge sheets. Some days it feels like the ward runs according to paperwork and processes rather than patients.

Fay will come up from the recovery room; I will start the routine observations, checking her blood pressure, pulse, and blood loss. I'll make sure she's pain-free, and generally feeling alright. If she still has intravenous fluids, I'll make sure they are running correctly. Then there's the baby. Check he or she is pink, warm, and well. Hopefully, the baby will have fed in recovery, but if not, I'll make sure Fay tries to feed. If all of this sounds process-driven and nurse-like, that's probably because it is. This part of the job is about ensuring physical wellbeing, making sure that the patient is post-operatively well. No matter how much I think that I never wanted to be a nurse, or that I don't want to care for patients who are unwell, there are aspects of the midwife's role that need me to have those skills.

I have to know how to carry out the nursing basics. That's not to say that I lose the "with woman" side of the role. Midwife. With woman. That's what the word means, and every time I think about my role, I remember that. I'm not doing this just to carry out the checks and write in the paperwork; I'm here because I want to make a better experience for each woman that I care for.

When Fay arrives on the ward, I meet the recovery midwife and the theatre assistant in the corridor, before they wheel the bed down into the space that I have prepared. Fay is tucked under a plain white sheet and a light blue waffle blanket. Just visible above the top of the covers is her baby, cradled in her arms. I smile at her, and peer to smile at her baby too.

"Hi Fay. I'm Violet. I'm a student midwife. I'll be taking care of you this evening," I say, as I walk down the corridor next to her bed.

"Hi," she replies. She seems alert. There's a metal pole at the top of the bed, with a hook at the top for her IV fluid bag. Just dangling below the blanket at the side of the bed is her catheter bag.

"She's exhausted," the recovery midwife tells me, after she has wheeled the bed into position. "It's been a long day."

Fay manages a weak smile and nods. "You can say that again."

The theatre assistant sets up the drip onto one of our free-standing poles and tucks the baby into a cot by Fay's bedside. Meanwhile, the recovery midwife runs through the handover.

"She's had some stitches for the forceps. The caesarean itself was straightforward when we got there. Record time, I think." She shows me the operation notes and pulls out the drug chart. "She's had the usual PR analgesia, and the drip is to stay up until this bag has run through, then you can take it down. Post op, everything was fine. Baby was a little slow to pick up, but we gave a little oxygen, and she was fine. No grunting. Had a little breastfeed, but not for long. Probably needs to try again before the end of shift." She pauses for a moment, as if running through a checklist in her head, trying to work out if she has forgotten anything. "Partner has been with her all day. He left about half an hour ago, but I told him that he can pop in and see her later."

"Thanks," I say, taking the brown folder containing Fay's notes. It's strange to think that a caesarean can be normal and straightforward, especially one that was performed in an emergency situation, but that's the way it is. Not everyone comes into hospital and has a natural vaginal birth, but I never thought that midwifery would be all catching babies and getting to cuddle them afterwards. Postnatal ward gives me plenty of opportunities for those cuddles, but it is also teaching me about how much nursing is necessary as part of my role.

I put the notes down onto the bedside cabinet as the midwife and assistant wheel the spare bed back to theatre and leave Fay in my care.

"Sounds like you've had a tough day," I say.

She looks exhausted. I can't begin to

imagine what it is like being in labour all day, and then having to go through an operation. On top of that, having a baby to look after seems like an impossible task. Even though I can't imagine, I can empathise, and I can care.

"Do you think you can manage a cup of tea?"

Her face brightens up. "Am I allowed one? Oh yes, please." It's as though I have offered her something far more exciting than a simple drink. Sometimes it's the little things that make all the difference.

When I have made the tea, I will come back and talk to her, be with her, listen to whatever she wants to tell me about her birth day. I will support her to feed her baby, and I will make sure she is comfortable and well. Most of all, I will be with her, because that is why I'm doing this: to be with woman.

Chapter Thirteen

Even though there are always lots of women and babies to care for, and I'm on my feet for most of the day, postnatal ward is not necessarily more tiring than any of the other placements, so far. Perhaps it is because there is a routine to the day that everything flows in a natural order. Still, by the end of the fourth week, I'm exhausted. Maybe it's working whilst trying to complete my assignments for the term. Maybe it's not just that.

Since Zoe and Luke got it together, things have felt different. I mean, I knew that it wouldn't be the same, it couldn't be, but I didn't know exactly what it was going to be like. I hope that now they are starting to go out on dates and act more like a "normal" couple that feeling might start to settle.

When I get home after my early shift on Saturday, I have the first chance in two days to talk to Zoe. I get home from my placement just after three in the afternoon, and I can't wait to see her. The house is silent when I open the front door, and when I look into her room it's empty. My disappointment feels like biting into a sweet, thinking it's going to be sugary in the centre and finding out it's sour. There's no Luke, and even Carl doesn't seem to be around. I make a drink, and pull two chocolate biscuits from a pack, think again, and take a third. Why not?

It's not often that the house is quiet and unoccupied; there's usually someone in the living room or the kitchen to talk to. Today, I make do with taking myself up to my room, and flop onto my bed to enjoy my snack and occupy myself with a book until Zoe gets home.

I'm not patient enough, and I send her a text.

Home now. WUU2? xx

I hate myself for using the shorthand for "what are you up to?" as soon as I've typed it, but I press send before I waste time rewriting.

I put my phone down on the bed next to me and get stuck into the book I'm currently reading. It's a distraction. I used to love to read, and I guess I haven't had much time since I've been at uni. Still, it doesn't feel like a pleasure, it feels like a pacifier.

I've read two and a half chapters before I hear the front door click open. I set down my book and try to focus, and work out whether it is Zoe, and if so, whether she's alone.

"Violet?" It's Zoe's voice.

As soon as I hear her coming up the stairs I leap off my bed and spring to open my door to see her. I feel like a puppy who has been left for too long by her owner. Perhaps I shouldn't think about myself in such a negative, needy light, but it's the truth. I have become used to having Zoe here with me, accessible all day every day, and I have loved it.

Back home, growing up, our homes were a ten minutes' walk apart. Even then, I would see her every day. I can't imagine a time when I won't be able to be with her. It's hard to explain without making it sound weird. It sounds like a cliché, but she truly is like the sister that I never had. It's not like the sentiment has been one-sided. Our bond runs both ways.

Yesterday she was up and off to her placement before I was out of bed, and I wasn't home until after ten. She was already asleep. Today it was my turn to be out of the house whilst she was still snoring. If this is what I'm like about time with Zoe, how am I ever going to have a *relationship* while I'm studying. How will I ever manage it when I'm a midwife?

Zoe manages to get to the landing before I throw my arms out and hug her.

"It's not been that long," she laughs, as she drops her bag onto the floor and joins the hug.

"Two days! And I have been waiting to hear about your date!" I have to laugh too, because the thought is ridiculous. How can I miss her presence after such a short time? I don't know, but I do. I always miss her.

"I texted you," she says, and it's true. We have messaged each other, but it's just not the same.

I shrug, and say, "Tell me everything! What have you been up to?" My voice is heavy with exclamation marks; if I really were that dog, I would be wagging my tail furiously, and probably licking her

117

cheek. I manage not to.

We go into her room. She tugs her jumper off and throws it onto her chair, and then lets her hair out of the high ponytail that she favours for work. I don't think she has to wear her hair tied back, it's her choice. I have to keep my hair up and my nails short and unpolished. The sacrifices we make for our careers.

"Seriously," I say. "What's new? How's everything going with Luke?"

"You don't have to be serious," she grins. "There's nothing to be serious about. He is lovely. Just as you would expect him to be." She starts to brush her hair. It falls in long, natural waves, shimmering like sunlight.

"Would I?" I ask.

"I suppose I imagined for quite a while what he would be like," she says. "And what I imagined is quite close to the truth." She pauses, before adding, "Which is great, because I thought that he was going to be wonderful."

That gets a big smile from me. She is positively radiant with happiness. I have never seen her like this before, and if Luke is the cause of this, then I can't be anything other than thrilled for her.

"Tell me about your date." If I don't have the time or inclination for my own love life at the moment, at least I can live vicariously through hers.

It's her turn to shrug.

"We walked into town and had dinner at that Mexican place opposite the park."

"The one with two-for-one cocktails?"

"You got it! But we had three cocktails each, I mean, why not, right?"

"Did you actually have dinner?" I take the brush from her and run it through her hair. This is something we used to do years ago. When we were younger we both decided that we wanted long hair, and our respective parents agreed to let us grow it out. I decided one day when I was about six years old that I was going to cut my fringe. I made such a hack job of it that instead of telling me off for it, my mum just felt sorry for me. Still, the only way to make me look half decent was to chop off the rest of my locks to match. After that I was fascinated

119

by Zoe's hair. She told me that she would get hers cut short to match mine, but I insisted that she didn't. Keep it, I told her. Don't you dare spoil it just because of me. She would have though. She would have done that for me. Even though I knew how much she loved her long hair, she would have let go of it in a flash for me. I lost mine through my own stupidity, or since I was only a child, let's call it misadventure.

"Are you even listening?" she says, putting her hand up and stopping me.

"I'm sorry." I haven't heard a word that she has been saying. "For some reason I was thinking about that time I cut my hair."

She bursts into a peel of laughter. "You wanted me to cut mine too!" she says, in between her giggles.

I frown and shake my head. "No, I told you not to."

She pauses for a moment, trying to hold in her laughter. "Oh maybe," she says. "You looked pretty cool with short hair though. I was probably jealous and wanted to have the same hair as you."

I shake my head, and laugh too, but at what she has said, rather than at the memory of the situation. "I looked like a boy."

"Short hair is cute," she says. "I would look terrible with short hair. I would just be all freckles and silly little snub nose. I *need* my hair to be pretty. You are naturally gorgeous."

I hand her the hairbrush back, and smile. "I'm not but thank you. It's you that has the lovely boyfriend and gets to go on dreamy dates. Tell me again. I'm listening."

"You could have a dreamy boyfriend and go on lovely dates too if you wanted to," she says. "I didn't think you wanted that though."

I shrug and say nothing. I probably don't. I don't think I do. I don't think I could anyway.

"We had dinner, and then we walked back through the gardens. It was dark by then. The park was beautiful, with all the Christmas lights, and the smell of doughnuts coming up from the skating rink. It was busy, you know. Lots of teenagers around, hanging about in their groups, playing music though the loudspeakers on their phones. I don't know why they do that. Luke had his arm around me, and we were like a little bubble, like no one else mattered. There were so many people, but it could have just been us."

I can feel the warmth inside me, as though I can share the feelings of love that she is experiencing.

"It sounds perfect," I say. My voice is quiet and soft, like it is coming from far away. "Zoe, I'm so happy for you."

Now we *are* being serious. The laughter has stopped, and the two of us are sitting, looking at each other, understanding that what she has is something bigger than either of us thought it was going to be.

"Thanks," she says. "Thanks, Violet. Thank you for giving me the push to finally do this. Thank you for encouraging me to go on normal dates. Thank you for everything that you have done and everything you do. I know that things are changing, that things are probably going to change even more, but whatever happens, you are so important to me."

"Oh Zo." I don't know what to say. There isn't anything that I can say.

"I was thinking, maybe we should

set some time aside that's just for us. So we know that we are always going to see each other, no matter what."

I'm about to say that it's difficult, with me being on shifts, but instead I think about all that she has done for me, and how important she is to me too.

"Yes," I say. "I'd love that."

"How about Mondays. Monday afternoon. We will commit to coffee and cake, and all the girlie chat that we can handle?"

I grin and nod. "All of my favourite things, with my favourite person. What more could I ask for?"

She holds her hand out, as if to shake on it, and seal the deal, but as I move forward, instead she grabs me, pulling me towards her, into another warm, deep embrace.

"I'll always be here for you," she says, her face buried in my hair. "I promise. Always."

"Me too, Zoe. Me too."

Chapter Fourteen

My first official Monday meet-up with Zoe comes at the end of a morning shift for me and a placement day for her. I'm tired, but grateful for the chance to sit and chat. I have a lot on my mind, and knowing that we have this time set aside has made me worry about it a lot less than I might have otherwise. I don't want to stress about interrupting her and Luke, or being in the way, bringing them down with my problems when otherwise they are obviously so incredibly happy. This time together feels like a safe space to talk.

The main thing that's bothering me is planning my SPOKE placements on the non-maternity units. I'm not looking forward to any of them. I know that I should probably be more positive, but, as I have said, I never wanted to be a nurse. It sounds terrible when I articulate it, but I don't really want to work with sick people. I can't make that sound anything other than terrible. Even though I have obviously come to realise how important it is to understand about the nursing elements of maternity care, actually going into nursing units or nursing wards is making my anxiety bubble inside me. Every time I start to think about planning my placements I feel physically sick.

I try to explain it to Zoe.

"I'm dreading the non-midwifery placements," I tell her. I'm pushing a fragment of carrot cake around my plate absent-mindedly, slightly disappointed that they had sold out of the Bakewell before we arrived.

Zoe looks at me quizzically. "It will be good experience for you, won't it? What's worrying you?"

I settle my fork down, and Zoe swoops in like an over-keen seagull to take my leftovers. I look up at her and manage a smile.

"Ill people," I say. It sounds dreadful coming out of my mouth. I pick up my mug and take a mouthful of mocha, trying to wash away the bad taste of the words.

Zoe laughs for a second, and then stops. "You're serious," she observes.

"Uh-huh," I say. "Awful, isn't it?"

She starts to shake her head but turns

the shake into a nod instead. "Maybe a little."

I fiddle with the fork, running my finger over the steel distractedly.

"Is it bothering you that much?" she asks.

Without looking at her, it's my turn to nod. "I feel so bad for thinking it, but I never wanted to be a nurse. I don't deal well with sick people. I don't know; I just don't think I'm the best person to be caring for people that are, you know, ill."

"But you have maternity patients that are ill, surely. It's not all happy endings, is it?"

I sigh and say, "You're right. I know. I feel like it's a bit of a waste of time though. I don't want to be a nurse, I don't want to focus on sickness, I want to be a midwife. It's like sending you on a placement to…to…" I can't think of an equivalent example.

"To a zoo, probably," Zoe smiles. "Although that might actually be quite useful."

She always manages to make me feel a little better. Still, as much as I feel bad for thinking the things I do, I can't get around the fact that this is the truth.

"Where do you have to go, exactly," she asks.

"I have to choose relevant areas. Places that are going to help me to learn how to be a better midwife. I would rather spend more time on my actual maternity placement learning how to be a better midwife."

"Children's ward might be nice," she says. Then she stops to think. "Actually, no. It would probably be awful. I don't know. I pictured brightly coloured walls and clowns going in to cheer up the children and…well, I suppose it's not like that at all. Looking after children that are so unwell that they need to be in hospital is probably very demanding, isn't it?"

I nod again, slowly and silently. I thought something similar when we were told about the allocations, and it took me about the same amount of time as it did for Zoe to understand that it wasn't going to be a kids' party.

"Mental health?" she ventures. "That's not the same as a nursing ward.

127

Could be interesting."

I shake my head almost reflexively. "Oh no."

I'm not sure what would happen in a mental health unit. The only experience I have is from television and the media, and I doubt very much that modern mental health treatment is anything like *One Flew Over the Cuckoo's Nest*. I hope it's not, anyway. I have my own mental health issues to deal with. How would I be able to support other people, patients that should be getting care from a trained professional rather than an anxious student midwife? I feel like I would be doing them a disservice by being involved in their care.

"I don't know how to look after people with those kinds of complex needs," I say. "I imagine it would be a ward full of people who are in need of a lot of support. It would be heart-breaking."

"Not as heart-breaking as being on a ward full of children with serious diseases without a cure," Zoe says.

I can feel tears prickling my eyes. If thinking about the placements is able to upset me this much, what am I going to be like when I have to start attending them.

"Listen," Zoe says. She wipes away the tear that's formed in my eye. "You need to try to get as much as you can out of these placements. Look for positives. Try to think of things that you can apply to midwifery. Think about those women that you care for that are going to be ill, and how applying yourself in these placements will benefit them."

"We have women with high blood pressure, postnatal haemorrhages, gestational diabetes," I say. "If I go onto the medical wards to look after people with raised blood pressure or diabetes I'll probably end up stuck with a bunch of old people…" I stop myself before I say anything else, as I realise what I must sound like.

"Ill people can be pregnant, and pregnant people can be ill though, surely." It's obvious when she says it.

"I don't see many of them. I mean, I haven't so far, but sure, of course that's true."

I've thought about everything from my own perspective. I don't want to be a nurse. I don't want to look after ill people. I don't want to look after old people. Nursing isn't my vocation. I'm sure that the women I will meet who have serious illnesses or medical conditions won't want to have them either. I need to look beyond what I want and focus on becoming the best midwife that I can be.

I know Zoe is trying to help, and I know she is trying to make me feel better about the placements, but I'm stepping out of my comfort zone, and as soon as I do that my anxiety starts to rear its ugly head. I've been so in control. I thought I was over it. I thought I could do this. Now, I think that I was deluding myself.

I can't talk about it anymore, so I smile and nod, and change the subject.

It's two weeks until the start of Christmas break. I don't know if it is too soon for Zoe and Luke to want to spend the holiday together. If it were me, I would think it was too soon. She hasn't mentioned it, though. I segue into the topic.

"I'll sort it all out after Christmas," I say. I add, as if it's an afterthought, "Have you talked to Luke about the holidays."

She acts as though it's a reasonable change in conversation, so I can't have sounded as clunky as I felt.

"He's going back to Leeds; I'm going home to the folks. Same as usual." She doesn't look at all upset by the prospect of their enforced separation.

"And you're okay with that?" I ask.

"Sure. It's early days. Family comes first," she says. Then she rests her hand onto mine and adds, "And friends."

Three weeks at home, back in Portland, with Zoe. The two of us alone together again. It really is going to be a good Christmas. Whatever happens next term can wait. I'm not going to think about it. I'm going to enjoy the holidays, and my time with my friend.

Chapter Fifteen

Despite the extra time that I have with Zoe, being home for Christmas break feels different to any of our previous holidays. If it were Easter or maybe even summer, we might have stayed at Tangiers Court, Zoe, Luke, and I, but as she said Christmas means family, and family means home.

Of course, Zoe has been messaging Luke constantly over the holidays. It's not like she has been stuck to her phone the whole time, but every time her Samsung has pipped out its three little beeps, she has scrambled to look at the screen. I can tell that she has been trying hard not to let her budding relationship with Luke affect the time she has with me, but still it has. I don't think badly of her. If I had a boyfriend, or anything like one, I would probably want to be messaging him too. Especially if he happened to be a few hundred miles away.

Even on the way back to university, her phone has been ringing out the signal to herald more messages from Luke.

She's the driver; I still don't have my licence, but I'm a good passenger - I brought a bag of sweets for the journey after all.

"He should be there when we get back," she tells me.

I nod, and realise she is looking at the road and not at me. "Okay," I say. It sounds flat and disinterested, and I don't want her to think I'm bored. "You must be looking forward to seeing him. Have you got anything planned together?"

I want the answer to be no. Selfish as it might sound, I've had Zoe to myself for the past three weeks, and it has felt like things have been normal between us again. All the time though, I knew we would be coming back, and I knew she was going to be spending her time with him instead. When I think about it like this, it sounds awful. I have to stop this. I have to let her get on with her life, and more importantly, I have to get on with mine.

It's Friday afternoon. We don't have to be back at uni until Monday, but Luke is coming home today, and so we are too. Home. It's strange how I think of Tangiers

Court as home now, rather than Portland, where I spent Christmas with my mother. I would have always called there *home* until recently. Portland is half an hour's drive from the university, it's not like I left home and travelled the world in search of adventure. Zoe and I moved away but stayed as close to home as possible. It's an adventure, but it's a safe one. They are, apparently, my favourite kind.

"I guess you'll be busy tonight then." The sentence comes out a lot harsher than I mean it to. I don't want to burst Zoe's bubble. I wished and hoped for her and Luke to get together, after all. I've had the luxury of having her to myself, if you exclude the phone calls and messages; now it's time to give her back.

She takes her eyes off the road for a split second and flashes me a look of concern.

"I don't mean -" I start to apologise.

She looks away, focusing on the duel carriageway ahead of us.

"I'm sorry," I say. "I've enjoyed having the holidays with you. I want you to be happy, you know that."

She remains tight-lipped and nods silently.

I turn my head and look out of the passenger window. The sky is a pale washed-out grey. The fields that we are driving past are a dull dark green in the winter afternoon light. Every so often the background is broken up by the occasional off-white dots of sheep. The whole scene appears depressed and dreary, but there is still an underlying beauty to it, which reminds me of why I would never want to live far from here. We head along the road in silence, and as we crest a hill I know that if I look across and through Zoe's window I will be able to see the slightest glimpse of the sea.

When I look over, I see a stream of tears on Zoe's cheek.

"Zoe. Zoe, what's up? I'm sorry. Gosh, really, I didn't mean anything. Please. Look, pull over, don't, please." Despite the January cold, I suddenly feel very hot. I want her to stop the car, I need it as much for myself as for her.

"I'm fine," she says. Her words sound fragile.

"You're obviously not. Zo, I'm so happy for you and Luke, I honestly am. I don't want to get in the way of -"

"You are not in the way. You will never be in the way."

She flicks on her indicator and pulls over into a lay-by, bringing us to a sharp stop. Then, she turns as far as her seatbelt will allow, and she looks at me.

"I have missed Luke so much, but I'm scared. I'm scared of not being able to spend as much time with you as I want to. I'm scared that, because Luke lives with us, I'm always going to be under some kind of pressure to be with him, to talk to him, to prioritise him - and most of all I'm scared because I don't want to do that. The past few weeks, I have felt awful when you and I have been shopping and he has phoned up, or when we have been in the coffee shop and he has texted. You know, all those times when it would usually just have been the two of us." She is still crying, perhaps even more now. The tears are silent, but they are running down her face, through her light peach-coloured blusher, leaving thin grey trails in their wake.

"Zoe. It's okay. It's alright. We will work it out. It is going to be fine."

I nod my head towards the rear-view mirror, and she looks up, seeing her reflection. She sniffs a snotty laugh and reaches for a tissue.

"Can't be turning up looking like a sad clown, can I?" She tries to smile.

"Please don't worry about me, Zoe. Whatever happens, I'm always going to be around. I will always be your best friend. Always. Or at least for as long as you want me to be."

"I always want you to be," she says, and somehow this tilts her over the edge again. She honks out a deep sob and I reach over and wrap my arms around her. Anyone driving past would wonder what on earth we are doing here, but, as usual, when it comes to me and Zoe, I just don't care what anyone thinks. All I care about is us.

As Luke predicted, when we get to Tangiers Court just before three, he is already back. Not only that but he has picked up some food from the supermarket, and there is a box of donuts on the work surface in the kitchen next to the kettle.

"I brought the snacks, you can make the tea," he smiles, and scoops Zoe up into a welcoming hug.

"Or you two can hug and I will comfort eat them all," I say. I flash them my biggest grin so that they know I'm joking, but the chocolate-glazed treats do look amazing. "How was Christmas?" I ask, as Zoe nuzzles her head into Luke's chest.

"Great, yeah, thanks. Christmas can't be anything other than great, can it?" Luke says.

He doesn't say that he missed Zoe or couldn't wait to get back here. I don't know why I expected that to be his answer, I suppose because that is what Zoe would have said if I asked her. Christmas *is* always great, but she looks so much happier now than she has for the entirety of the past three weeks.

This is home now, and Luke is her happiness.

Chapter Sixteen

Last term was a relative breeze. I was back in a clinical placement that I'd been to before, my assessments were all written assignments. I felt confident and competent. I think it was just what I needed to consolidate what I learned last year - not just about midwifery, but also in terms of my self-confidence and ability to handle situations. If I thought that I'd conquered my anxiety though, I was very wrong. Did I think that? Did I ever really think that?

The night before the start of my second term, Luke and Zoe are watching a movie downstairs, and even though I know I am more than welcome to join them, I feel like getting ready for my classes, and having some alone time. Carl is out somewhere, so I'm sitting on my bed with a stack of papers that I printed out on my mum's computer. I've got the module guides for this term: 'Pharmacology' and 'Complex Midwifery Care'. I knew this was coming. Complex Midwifery Care is the module that I have been dreading, for the assessment rather than the subject itself. This term I will have my second Objective Structured Clinical Examination.

My anxiety spiralled out of control when I had the first OSCE last year. I ran from the skills lab without being able to carry out the assessment and failed without even trying. I can't do that to myself again.

If that's not scary enough, I also have a written examination for the pharmacology module. I'm not a mathematician, not by a long shot. My brain is scientific enough to understand the biology and biochemistry required of me for the course and for my future career, but maths is not my strong point. I know that it's essential that I can calculate the correct doses of drugs and administer them safely to mothers and babies, but this module is filling me with fear. I don't know how I'll be able to get through it.

I check through the module guide. There is no room for error with this exam. I have to answer every question correctly. That sounds incredibly harsh. How can an exam have a one hundred percent pass mark? Perhaps there has been some kind of mistake. I will have to ask the module leader. I keep reading. At least if I fail this exam I will be able to resit. Once.

My hand is starting to shake, and I let the paper fall onto the bed. I feel sick. I shouldn't have started to think about these modules. Then again, it's better that I think about them and get this out of my system while I'm in the comfort and privacy of my bedroom instead of flipping out in the middle of the classroom.

I close my eyes, and bring my knees up to my chest, hugging them against me. Maybe I should forget about this for tonight and go and sit with Zoe and Luke instead. I could grab a cup of tea and some chocolate and switch my brain off. It almost feels like a possibility, but as I sit here, thinking, my thoughts keep flicking back to the OSCE.

I passed last year, but only on my second attempt. I could have messed up my entire career - my entire future - because of a stupid panic attack. I failed myself. I let myself down. That's what happened. The sickness in my stomach is rising through me now. I'm glad that I am sitting down already, because I feel like I'm on a rocking ship on a rough tide rather than seated on my bed. I haven't felt like this for months, and I sure as heck haven't missed this feeling.

No, I didn't think that I'd conquered my anxiety. I don't believe that I could ever be that overconfident. I managed to push it away into a dark corner for a little while, but it has still been there, waiting to resurface. Perhaps this is why I was tense and snappy with Zoe. It wasn't about coming back here and not being able to spend time with her; it was about knowing what was in store for me this trimester. I knew that the OSCE was drawing near. I know that it is - and it terrifies me.

I kick my legs and thrash them against the pile of paperwork, pushing the sheets onto the floor. I want them away from me. I don't want to think about it anymore. I can't. It's too much.

My face is burning hot, my cheeks on fire with the heat of anxiety. I pick up my phone from beside me and look at the time. It's only half past eight. Too early to sleep, but I don't want to go downstairs now. Zoe will know that there is something wrong, and she will stop watching her film, take me into the kitchen or bring me up here, and sit and talk me down until I'm feeling calm, in control, and terribly guilty about taking her away from what she is doing. I have to do this by myself. Zoe isn't going to be as available for me as she has been, and the sooner I start to deal with that, and accept it, the better.

I didn't realise how much that thought would affect me.

I pull in a long deep breath and let out a sob, then cover my mouth immediately. I was too loud. I don't want to distract her. I don't want to be any trouble. I'm terrible, I'm useless. Why shouldn't she be able to get on with her life without having me in the way?

I hear the living room door open downstairs, and Zoe shouts up to me. "Are you alright?"

I call back, "Yeah, thanks. I had my headphones on. I was getting carried away."

"Okay," she says. She would never usually have accepted such an obvious lie. She must be having a good night.

"I'm going to get in the bath," I

shout. "Have fun!"

I hadn't actually thought about getting into the bath before I said the words, but my brain usually knows what my body needs, or vice versa.

"Alright." One word, and then she's silent.

I hear the downstairs door click closed again. I feel strange. Not just because of the anxiety that is bubbling inside me; I feel like something has definitely changed between Zoe and me. Before Luke, she would have run upstairs, checked on me and not taken my shouted words for an answer. She would have talked to me until I spilled all of my thoughts and feelings.

Perhaps I *have* been too dependent upon her. Perhaps this is actually for the best for both of us. I have to start learning how to deal with my thoughts. I have to get in control of my own life, and let Zoe live hers.

I stretch out my arms, throwing them as wide as I can, and then kick my legs forward again. It's kind of like a seated star jump; all I want to do is to push some of the stress out of my limbs. I also want to shout out, or maybe even scream, but given the

144

circumstances, I control myself.

Instead, I get up, pull my robe off the hanger, and head along the corridor to the bathroom. If there is one thing I know for sure, it's that feeling hot water embrace me will make me feel at least a little better - even if it is only temporary.

This term is going to be tough, and I'm going to have to be tougher. More importantly, I'm going to have to learn how to do it without Zoe.

Chapter Seventeen

The first day of term always seems to be a jumble of emotions. There's the thrill of being introduced to new modules and looking forward to what I will be learning during the sessions, and the excitement of catching up with my course mates again after a few weeks away from each other. On the other hand, new modules mean more assignments to prepare for and worry about.

I already know what this term has in store, and there is not much that I'm looking forward to. There's the pharmacology exam, the second OSCE, and I can't even balance my dread of these with the happy anticipation of my placement, because I know that I need to get at least some of my SPOKE sessions over with. I probably shouldn't think of them like that. I have been so negative about the external visits I have to attend, but to me, they feel like challenges rather than opportunities. Psychologically, not having as much time with Zoe is no doubt making all of my worries about this term even worse.

Still, it's Monday. That means when we have finished our lectures for the day instead of heading back to Tangiers Court, we will go into town for our weekly mate date. Zita Somerville is leading the Monday morning module this term, but even though she is one of the most inspirational and engaging tutors, my mind is still wandering to this afternoon, cake and, above all, Zoe.

All the other students are full of passion and enthusiasm, but I'm starting to feel out of my depth. It's like I have been treading water, kicking my legs as hard as I can to try to keep afloat, but my head is starting to sink beneath the surface. I'm not as smart as any of my classmates. Everything comes so easily to them, not just retaining information and building on their knowledge, but their basic self-confidence far outweighs my own. I never put my hand up in class to answer anything because I'm terrified of being wrong, or more specifically, saying something stupid.

Zita is leading the pharmacology module, and she is currently standing by the side of the SMART board, talking us through the module guide.

"Why is it important for midwives to know about drugs?" she asks.

I instinctively look away from her. Not only do I not want to raise my hand, but also I don't want her to make eye contact with me and single me out. I have some ideas as to what the answer is, but I don't have the confidence to speak up.

One of the girls on the front row responds. "So that we understand what doctors are talking about."

There's a murmur of laughter, but it's amusement at the comment; no one is laughing at the girl, no one thinks she is stupid. I'm sure if I'd given that answer, I would have sounded ridiculous.

Even Zita smiles. "That is certainly one way of looking at it. We need to know what drugs are being offered to or prescribed for the women in our care. As advocates for women, knowing about the drugs that are used will help us to talk to them about the risks and benefits, and the side effects. Anything else?"

"We need to know about dosage?" Sophie speaks from my right. Her voice is uncertain, and she phrases her answer like a

148

question, but at least she has the confidence to say something.

"Especially if we are the ones that are giving the medication to the patient," Zita says. "In this module we will look at the most common drugs that are used, and you need to start making a mental note when you are in your placements, so that the usual dosages become second nature to you. There are many drugs that you will be able to give without them being prescribed by a doctor, because they are covered by the standing order for the unit. Make sure you know what is covered in your own hospital." She pulls a booklet from her bag and holds it in the air. "You will all need to read this document. You can access it online, and the address is in your module guides."

I recognise it. I've already read through it, but I know that I will have to revisit it several times before all of the content sinks in. It's the Nursing and Midwifery Council's *Standards for Medicines Management* guideline: the definitive principles from the midwifery regulatory body.

This all felt overwhelming when I

was preparing for the term last night, and today it is almost too much for me. I know that I still have so much to learn about the clinical elements of midwifery, but at least I vaguely understand what I'm doing and why I am doing it. The principles of pharmacology and medicines management are far more difficult to get my head around. If I make even the slightest error it could have huge implications. I guess that's why student midwives can only ever administer medication under supervision. We aren't expected to be experts, at least not yet, but in order to pass this module, I need to know enough to pass the exam.

After class, I leave the lecture block and walk out into a torrential downpour of rain. Zoe is standing across the path, sheltering beneath the overhang at the front of the library.

I don't have a hood or an umbrella, so I try to pull my jacket up over my head, and dash over to join her.

"Typical," she says. She looks at me and her face registers concern. "You okay? What's up?"

I hadn't meant to let my feelings show through. I wanted our time together to be light and happy, but sometimes my emotions are too big for me to stuff them into a corner, out of view.

"I don't think I can do it," I say.

My face is already dripping wet from the rivulets of rain, and I could probably get away with letting my tears out, but still, I try to hold them back.

"You still want to go into town?" she asks.

"Uh, yes, of course." The very thought that I might have jeopardised our coffee date makes a heavy leaden feeling thud into my gut. "Don't you?"

"I mean, do you want to stay here and talk instead? We could go into the bar?"

"Oh, right." It's always my instinct to think the worst, but I should never jump to the conclusion that Zoe would let me down or not want to talk to me just because of my own stupid thoughts. I feel even more of an idiot now.

It's early. First day back at lectures, are there going to be that many students in the bar at half past four?

151

"If it's not too busy," I say.

She nods. "Hey. It's going to be okay."

I couldn't stop my tears after all. I give her a weak nod in reply, and wipe at my eyes.

"Come on. Let's go and find a quiet corner and a strong drink."

"Strong coffee is fine for me," I say. The last thing I need when I'm already feeling down is alcohol.

We both pull our jackets above us, making a run for the main university block that houses the union bar.

Five minutes later we are sitting in the almost empty room that I've previously only seen packed with boisterous students. It feels strange being here when it is so quiet, almost like we are trespassing. Still, I much prefer it this way. I would rather have made it to our planned destination and be sitting with a slice of something sweet and sticky and a latte that doesn't taste like instant, but at least I'm here with Zoe.

We've hung our coats up on the backs of two chairs, and we're sitting next to each other on two others. It's like we have two spaces reserved for friends who have popped out somewhere. Strangely it reminds me of the absence of the two house mates that are always around us these days.

"What's happened, Violet?" she asks, her eyes heavy with concern.

I shake my head. "I don't know where to start," I say.

"I thought everything was getting better. You haven't seemed at all anxious recently." She is about to blow onto her cappuccino - there are no mochas available in the union bar, apparently - when she stops and looks at me. "I haven't noticed, have I? You've been worrying and I haven't noticed. Oh, Violet. Oh...I'm so sorry." She puts her cup back down onto its saucer and reaches over for my hand. "I really am sorry."

"You shouldn't have to look out for me and worry about me all the time," I say. "It's not your job to be my minder. Or my carer."

"It's not like that. I didn't mean -" She stops again. "You know I don't mean that."

153

Objectively I know she would never mean that, but beneath my anxiety-tinted glasses everything looks dark. My brain can make me believe almost anything.

"It's all getting on top of me. Last term - I think it gave me a false sense of security. There was nothing big and scary, and I let myself get too comfortable."

She's giving me her full attention. I thought this was what I wanted, but now I feel guilty for my dependence upon her.

"Look," I say. "Let's talk about something else. I want to hear about what you have been doing. Tell me about your course. How is -"

She cuts me off. "You don't have to do that," she says. "Stop it. You don't need to hold back what you're feeling or worry about offloading onto me. We can talk about what I have been doing later. I'm fine. I'm great, in fact. Apart from one thing."

"What's that?" I ask. This could be my chance to give something back, do something for her for a change.

She smiles and taps her spoon against the edge of my mug. "I'm worried about you, silly."

I was wrong. There doesn't appear to be much I can do about that.

"So, tell me," she says. "What happened today to make you feel like this?"

"It's not just today. I have exams this term, and I keep thinking about how I messed up last year. Then there's the SPOKE placements. We've already talked about them though; I don't want to bore you with all that again."

"You never bore me," she says. I know that she is telling the truth, because her eyes are filled with a mixture of concern and compassion. "You passed your OSCE resit, remember. You breezed through it. You can do that again."

"Breeze through a resit?" I say, with the faintest hint of a smile. I know what she means, and I know that her intentions are good, but it isn't as easy as she thinks. "I fluked it. I somehow managed to have a good day and -"

"Don't do that." She narrows her eyes, and her voice is sharp and serious. "Stop it."

But I can't. I can't change the way that I think about myself, not just because

155

she says so. Instead, I stop talking.

"Vi." She tries to get me to look at her, but my focus is transfixed upon the mug in front of me. If I look at her again I think I might start crying again. I don't want that. I don't want to do it to her. I have to start taking responsibility for myself. I'm nineteen years old. I'm not a child anymore. I shouldn't expect her to babysit me.

"Violet." She says my name again, firmly, commanding my attention.

Slowly, I bring my gaze up to meet hers.

"I need to do something about it," I say. "I have to get over this once and for all."

Her expression changes like a sharp snap. "You mean -"

She doesn't want to say it and I'm not sure that I do either. I have to though. I have to say the words to make them real.

"I'm going to make an appointment at the health centre." Actually forming the words and releasing them feels cathartic. "I'm going to get some support. Some drugs. Some...anything."

I hope that she won't blame herself

or think that I'm doing this because she can't give me all the time that she did before. It's not like that though. It's my anxiety telling me that. I know. Objectively, I know. I have to keep reminding myself, whilst I can still think objectively at least.

"I'm -" She pauses, trying to find the words. "I'm proud of you. I hope you don't take that the wrong way. I mean it in the best way possible. I know how difficult it must be. I know what it was like before, and I know how hard it is."

She does. She is the only person who does, because she has been there through everything. It's about time I was there for myself.

"If you want me to come with you, or anything, you know I will," she says.

"Thanks," I say.

I already know that I'm going to go alone. Having someone as dependable as Zoe has made me dependent. Now, I have to learn how to depend upon myself. The first step is to believe in myself and get my anxiety in check.

Chapter Eighteen

I make the appointment straight away, so that I don't give myself the chance to change my mind. I've coasted along for so many years, avoiding facing up to the fact that actually, I do need help. Zoe has been a crutch, and now that she is getting on with her life, I need to learn to walk on my own.

The meeting with the GP is not what I expected. It's nothing like the grim discussion I had as an eleven-year-old child, being dragged into the doctor's office by my parents. Then, the two of them pointed the finger of blame at each other for the full length of my assessment session, each convinced that the other was at fault for my anxiety. Meanwhile, I sat in silence, becoming more and more anxious. Looking back, I think that one of the main reasons that I didn't engage with treatment - the talking, counselling side of the treatment - was that I couldn't bear spending that extra time listening to my parents fighting. It was bad enough at home. If they were going to let their hostility spill over into the waiting room, I had to do everything I could to avoid that.

Now, things are different. Now, I'm an adult, and I can make my own decisions. I can make my own appointment, and I can look for support on my own terms. It's almost as though I'm actually too confident now to need help with my anxiety. Almost. I am confident enough to know that I need help.

So, here I am, face to face with Doctor Fisher, one of the three GPs that work in the campus health centre.

She starts with the standard questions about why I have come to see her. It feels strange being the patient. I'm starting to get used to being in the role of the professional, even though I'm still only at student level. I'm used to asking the questions, taking the history, thinking about what steps I need to take. Now, I'm giving my own history. I'm self-conscious; I feel like my every word will be judged.

"I should have seen someone sooner," I say. "I have suffered too long. I mean, it's been going on for too long. Eight years now, more or less. I started having anxiety attacks not long after I turned eleven. Things were bad at home, between my parents." She is watching me, nodding, saying nothing. "They didn't do anything to me. They didn't hurt me. Nothing like that. At least, you know, they didn't physically hurt me, or neglect me or anything. But -" I pause again.

I don't know what to say. They argued in front of me every day. My dad, in particular, said terrible things to my mother. She sometimes responded, but after he hit her a few times she stopped arguing back. I don't want to talk about that though. I don't want to talk about the reasons that this started, I want to look for a way to make it end.

"They're divorced now. I live here, not at home. I don't want to blame them for what happened then. I want to stop feeling like this."

Doctor Fisher nods. "Why didn't you get help before?"

"I wasn't ready," I say. The words come out without me having to think about them too much, and I believe that they are the truth. "I didn't think I needed help. I

160

thought that I would get better. But I haven't. I could have a better life if I didn't feel the way that I do. I want to pass my course. I want to be the best I can be. To do that I need to try to fight this."

Do I blame them? Do I really blame my parents for making me feel this way? I always thought that I would miss my mum awfully when I started university. I'm all that she has now that she and Dad have divorced, but still, I barely even message her. I see her at holidays, but I'm always eager to get away again. I don't want to feel like that. I don't want to enjoy the distance between us. Perhaps I also blame her for my inability to hold down a relationship. I'm too young to know that yet, to know it for sure, but I have the sneaking suspicion that I'm building a wall to protect myself, and to keep everyone out.

I don't want to be a Rapunzel in a tower, waiting for someone to come and rescue me. I would rather be Snow White, having a long nap in a glass case. I realise that still means not letting anyone get too close.

"You tried drug treatment in the

past?" Fisher asks.

I nod. "I don't want that again. At least, not what I had before."

"Side effects?"

Again, I nod. "I felt out of it all of the time. It was horrible. I preferred the anxiety to the apathy."

"Okay," she says. "We can try something different. Not everyone experiences those side effects, and not every drug will make you feel like that." She taps a few keys on her computer and turns back to me. "What are your thoughts on counselling?"

"Does it help?" I ask.

"Some people, yes. Many people. You have to want to do it. If you can commit to the process, then, yes, it can help."

I think it over for a silent minute.

"Maybe," I say.

If I'm finding it strange being a patient here in this setting, how am I going to feel sitting with a counsellor for an hour every week. Besides, I know what is wrong with me, don't I? I know when this started and what caused it. Is rehashing all of that going to help me to feel any better?

"There's a waiting list, unfortunately. It's around twelve weeks at the moment. We have a lot of students who need support, and the service is stretched, I'm afraid."

I nod. I understand what it must be like. That's the other side to working in the health profession, you soon realise how the balance of supply and demand doesn't match up. People need services, but the services either don't exist, or the waiting list is so long that the treatment or support isn't much use by the time they get it.

"I could go on the list," I say, "and start the drugs now?"

"I would recommend that, yes," she says.

She seems like the sort of person that I can talk to. She is warm and caring, and she is talking to me on her level. I hope that I come across like this to the women that I care for.

"Okay," I say.

It's a no-brainer. I came here to get help, and if the help that is available now is drug treatment, then I have to give it a try. I can't carry on the way I have been. I have to do this now. It's for the good of my future. It's what I need.

I wish I'd accepted Zoe's offer of coming with me, sometimes just the moral support of having her by my side can make all the difference. She has Luke to think about now. I can't spend my whole life hanging around her neck. This is what is best for me, what is best for her, what is best for everyone. It is time.

Chapter Nineteen

Doctor Fisher warned me that the medication might not start working straight away, but I want to feel the effect as soon as possible. It took me this long to make the move and see a doctor, now I want to keep the momentum going. I can't expect a miracle cure. I'm not going to take a few pills and be a different person, but I hope that the drug treatment, the therapy sessions, and my own positive attitude will be steps in the right direction.

My exams are looming, and if I can at least get my mind under control and not flip out over them that will be something.

By the time I get back to the wards, two weeks after I start my meds, I can't decide if they are making any difference or not. My allocated placement for this term is antenatal ward, but I know that I have to start fitting in my SPOKE placements. On the first day with my mentor Becky, we sit over lunch and discuss the options available to me.

I have a shortlist of units and wards

that I think are likely to be useful. Becky reads through them as we sit in the office with our sandwiches.

"We can definitely get you into the Early Pregnancy Unit," she says. "Doctor St. Claire runs a clinic there, so we can ask her when she does the ward round."

Melanie St. Claire is one of the more approachable consultants. We see most of the consultant teams every day, as they carry out ward rounds for the antenatal patients. Doctor St. Claire always makes time to talk to the women, and she always makes time to talk to me.

I nod and smile. "That will be great."

"Same for the genito-urinary and gynae wards. Should be easy to get you in there if there aren't too many students already."

The nursing students are allocated to the wards too, so I have to fit in around them, as well as trying to make the SPOKE placements fit around my own shifts here.

"Have you had any thoughts about other places you'd like to spend some time?"

My mouth is full of bread and ham,

166

and I chew and swallow, giving myself the chance to prepare an answer. The bottom line is that I don't really want to be on a ward with sick people. It might sound terrible but spending time on a nursing ward does not appeal to me at all. I can learn all I need to through my maternity placements.

"Not really," I say, eventually. "Maybe A and E."

I've watched enough hospital-based fly-on-the-wall television to know that an accident and emergency placement will probably be exciting. It's not your standard kind of nursing ward, for a start, and it's one of those places, pretty much like delivery suite, that you never know what is going to come through the doors.

"Okay," Becky says. "What do you think you will learn there to help with your midwifery?"

I shrug. "I just thought that I would see a lot of different things." I'm not sure this is a good enough answer, so I add, "And it will be useful to see the how the staff manage, you know, with all the patients, and such a range of, er, problems."

Becky nods. "It's not a trick

question. I'm sure it could be useful. What else?" She writes A and E onto my list.

I've covered all of the pregnancy related units and wards, and I added in the only other place that I thought might be interesting.

"Er, maybe family planning? Is there a contraception clinic or something?"

One of the conversations that midwives have in community before we discharge patients to health visitor care is about what contraception they are planning to use. Some of the women look at us as though they think they will never have sex again - bear in mind this is usually between a week and two weeks after they have given birth - but some of them are already asking when they can resume normal services, as it were.

Becky nods and writes.

"I have a suggestion," she says. "I know it's not your specialism, but have you considered going to the mental health unit?"

I let my expression hit my face before I can stop my feelings showing. Even though I don't want to spend time on a general nursing ward, I would prefer a month there to spending a day on a mental health unit. Not because I don't care, or because of any prejudice, but more because of my own mental fragility. I'm scared that I will see myself and my own anxiety reflected back at me. I'm not sure that I am strong enough to look at it.

"What's the matter?" Becky asks. She places her sandwich on top of the lid of the plastic box she brought it in, using it as a makeshift plate. Wiping her hands on a wet wipe, she reaches over to me. "Hey, what's wrong?"

I must look even more concerned than I thought.

"I don't know. I don't think I would be much good there. I would rather not go."

She nods slowly and looks at me. Her eyes are fixed on mine, as though she is trying to buoy me up.

"There's a mother and baby unit at the Linden Unit. I know that they take some of our students, and it really would be a good opportunity for you. You don't have to do a placement on the main unit, if that's what's bothering you?"

"I'm what's bothering me," I say,

beneath my breath. I know she won't be able to hear me, and when she asks me what I said, instead I say, "I don't know what's bothering me."

She looks at me as though she doesn't quite believe me but isn't going to make a big deal of it.

"You could go for one or two days?"

"Can I think about it?" I ask. I don't feel hungry anymore, and I put my own sandwich back into its bag.

"I was a patient there," Becky says, out of nowhere. "After I had my first."

"I didn't realise," I say.

I feel terrible. What must she think of me? She must feel like I'm dismissive of the unit, and how will that make her feel about having been a patient there. Still, she is telling me this voluntarily.

"They saved my life. They helped me when I was at my lowest point. I don't think I would have been able to be a mother without the care and support that I got in the unit."

"It must have been awful for you." I don't want to pry too deeply or ask for any more information than she wants to give me.

"It was. For me, and for my family. I think everyone was terrified. No one knew what to say to me. No one knew what to do."

I don't know if I would know either. Mental health is not exactly something I'm good at dealing with, my own especially. I'm trying though, at least I'm trying.

Perhaps Becky is right. If I spend some time in the mother and baby unit, maybe I will be able to make the difference to a woman who really needs the unit's help and support. If I can say that I have been there and seen for myself what is available, I will be able to reassure someone that I need to refer. I would never have thought about this unit as an option, but it is already starting to make perfect sense. Still, I need to know that I'm strong enough. I want to be able to give a hundred percent.

"I think it would be useful," I say, quietly. "I need to think about it, but yes. I think you're right. Thanks, Becky."

"Now eat your lunch. I don't want you fading away halfway through the shift," she smiles.

Chapter Twenty

When I get home, I sit at my desk and make a shortlist of contenders for my SPOKE placements. I'm trying to think about the positives, and the experiences that I might be able to have, but I still have that undercurrent of fear that I won't be any use to the patients. I don't want to be a burden on the staff or a liability to patient care. I'm going to start phoning around the units after my shift tomorrow, so I have set myself the task of making this list final today. It's more difficult than I thought.

Zoe is out with Luke this evening. The house is quiet, but the lack of company and the silence is distracting me. I don't want to sit here with my own thoughts, even if I do need to concentrate. Outside, the evening is still light. It's coming up to eight, but it's warm enough for me to throw on a sweater and take my list out to the garden.

Looking for inspiration, I send a text to the group chat I have with Ashley, Simon and Sophie.

Where are you going for your

SPOKEs?

The last messages we sent in the chat were about some television game show that Simon had discovered. I still haven't watched it, but Ash and Sophie seem to think it's the best thing ever. I should get more involved, make more of an effort. The only messages I have sent have been about coursework or placements. I hate to imagine what they must think of me.

I'm lost in my thoughts when the back-door swings open and makes a thucking sound. I shudder a look in its direction and see Carl standing in the opening.

"Mind if I join you?" he says.

It's weird. We are halfway through the year and he still asks before sitting, even though we talk to each other now more than ever before.

"Sure," I say.

The paper in front of me still only has a few jumbled ideas scrawled upon it. I need to commit myself, but I would rather have the distraction of talking to Carl.

My phone buzzes on the table, jerking onto the paper, and I reach forward to pick it up.

"Are you trying to work?" he asks, leaning over to look at what I have written. That word, 'trying' feels like it is loaded with meaning, the implication being that I'm not getting far at all. The scrappy note is evidence that I can't get away from.

"Uh, sort of."

There's no point in asking Carl, he can't help me make the decisions I need to. The text is from Simon, giving me a brief list of his choices. The truth is, I already know where I should be considering, I'm stalling because I don't really want to go anywhere but the maternity placements.

"I can be quiet, if you like?"

He's seated himself next to me, and now he's craning to see my phone screen.

"No, it's fine, really." I let out a heavy breath. "I have to choose some elective placements. Not long ones, just a day here and there, but -"

"You don't want to." He finishes my sentence, making me aware of how patently obviously my feelings must be.

"Yep. I mean nope. I mean, I don't want to."

My words are starting to jumble because my brain is losing its focus. Trying to plan these sessions is making me more anxious than I have felt in days. I thought the tablets would have started working by now. I'm not meant to feel this way.

Carl straightens himself up, and tilts his body towards me, turning all his attention in my direction. "Tell me about it."

"About what?"

"Whatever you like. Whatever is bothering you about the placements."

I wrinkle my brow. "Really? Why?"

He prods the note, and says, "You're not getting far, and it's obviously bothering you, so…" He shrugs rather than finishing the sentence, and then he adds, "And I'm not doing anything. Go ahead."

I never imagined that talking through my worries with Carl could be so therapeutic. Even though he doesn't know the first thing about the practicalities of my course or my placement, he listened attentively. He asked me about how I was feeling, and what I was thinking. It's the first time in a while that I have felt listened to.

Zoe is still not home by eleven, and I have another early shift tomorrow. I have to go to bed without talking my final choices through with her. Thanks to my chat with Carl, I'm *almost* happy about my decisions, and I'm definitely feeling a lot more positive in general about the placements.

Although we are free to choose the SPOKE placements that we want to attend, there is some guidance in our practice documents to make sure that we are including everything that we should. One of the required SPOKE placement visits is to spend time with a specialist midwife.

St. Jude's hospital, where I have my clinical allocation, is lucky to have several specialist midwives. There's a midwife who specialises in bereavement care, one who is an expert in domestic abuse, one whose focus is teenage pregnancy. I know that I can learn so much from all of them, and I'm sure that eventually each of them will be able to give me insight and experience.

For my placement I'm going to spend the day with the mental health specialist. I hope that I will be able to visit the Linden Unit and the mother and baby unit with the specialist midwife. I don't think I could face going alone, but this could be the ideal compromise. I want to learn, but I can't risk letting myself be overwhelmed. I can't risk letting patients down.

Chapter Twenty-One

My routine settles back into its cycles of shifts and study. From the messages in the group chat, I can tell that I'm not the only one who is daunted by the non-midwifery placements. Sophie and Ashley have both been dithering equally about where to opt for, and even Simon is nervy.

I feel a lot better about the SPOKE placements now that I have actually made my mind and started to arrange them. I'm calmer than I have been for some time, and I can't help but believe the tablets are actually starting to help me.

Most mornings when I'm on late shifts I come down to an empty house. Luke has taken to going into uni to study even when he doesn't have lectures. I guess he wants to get it out of the way so that he can spend his at-home-time with Zoe. She's out of the door by eight while she's in the school, so that only leaves Carl. I don't see much of him in the mornings. I tend to treat myself to a lie in and lounge around in my room.

Today I went down to make tea and toast and found a distinct lack of milk. I've just bundled back in from my trip to the shop and flicked the toaster on when Carl hovers in. I say hover, because he is standing beside me in the kitchen, saying nothing, but looking at me like he has something on his mind and doesn't know how to start.

"Uh, morning," I say.

I'm not sure whether to prompt him or let this go and take my breakfast upstairs as I had planned.

"Just about," he says. The clock on the microwave says 11:50. I didn't realise it was so late. Still, I have a couple of hours before I have to leave. Plenty of time to do the whole lot of nothing that I was going to do.

"You okay?" I say the words without thinking, and that's it, I've committed to a conversation.

"I feel really bad," he says. I believe him. He's shifting his weight from one foot to the other, looking anywhere but directly at me. He's usually so confident, but now, he looks nervous.

179

He continues. "The other day, I went into your room. I'm sorry. I shouldn't have. I had a cracking headache and I needed paracetamol. I thought you might have some."

I can't imagine what is coming next, but I feel my cheeks starting to glow.

"I saw something. Do you mind if we, er, talk about it?"

I have a terrible sense of unease. My stomach is trembling like a jelly. I can't say no, although I feel like I should.

"Uh, sure," I say. My inflection makes it sound like a question, but really it's an uncertain agreement.

"Shall we sit outside?" he asks.

"Okay." My voice remains hesitant and uncertain. I don't have a clue where this is going.

I look into the toaster, wondering whether to ask him to wait until I've made my breakfast, but somehow I'm swept along, and I hear the pop as I go out of the door.

Out in the garden, he pulls back one of the chairs for me, and when I'm seated, he takes the chair beside me.

180

He leans back, looking far more relaxed than I'm feeling right now.

"I know that we aren't very close friends," he says, "but I'm worried about you."

My mind is racing, trying to work out what it is that he saw. What could possibly have happened to make him worry?

"You don't need to be. I'm fine," I say.

"Remember before Christmas, when we went out for drinks."

I remember, but it isn't at the forefront of my memories. It's not like it's something I have gone over and over in my brain. Is he - does he have some kind of feelings that I haven't picked up on?

"Yes," I say. I want to leave the talking to him.

"You told me something. I don't know if you remember. You were, I mean you weren't really drunk, but you were drinking, and I thought maybe you could have forgotten that you had said anything."

What does this have to do with him going in my room? Did I say something I shouldn't have? Did I tell him I liked him? I mean he's not *bad* looking, and he seems -

"You have no idea what I'm talking about, do you?" he laughs. There's no meanness in it; he's not laughing at me. "It's okay."

He leans closer towards me, closer to the table, and reaches across, taking hold of my hand. It feels reassuring rather than awkward, like he is trying to connect with me. I'm not a huge fan of physical closeness with people I'm not emotionally close to, but this somehow feels fine. It's calming. I almost like it.

"You told me about your anxiety. That you have trouble with it."

Of course. It all starts coming back to me. There was hardly anything else personal that I told him about myself. I was trying not to make a bad first impression, if you could call it that after we had lived together for weeks before talking to each other properly.

I nod my head and instinctively look down at the table. My embarrassment at the subject makes me shut down. I'm going to have to talk to a counsellor about it soon though, I have to get used to opening up.

Can I open up to Carl though? To my housemate that I barely know?

"When I went in your room, I promise I wasn't snooping around. If I wanted to root through your drawers I'd do that when you were out of the house, right?"

He smiles, and after a tiny pause I smile back.

He continues, "I saw a packet of tablets on your desk. I thought they might be what I was looking for at first. Then I recognised them because they're the same ones that my mum used to take. They're for the anxiety, aren't they?"

"The anxiety? Yeah."

I feel relieved that all he saw in my room were my meds. He didn't read through my emails or check my internet browser history. Come to think of it, though, there's hardly anything shocking in either of those places. I'm a fairly straightforward, vanilla kind of girl. I'm not thrilled that he went into my room, but I believe his explanation. It makes sense.

"Violet, I know that anxiety is really tough, I know how bad it can feel, but you don't need those tablets. They are no good

183

for you."

My forehead corrugates into a frown.

"I've struggled for a long time," I tell him. "I've suffered with this ever since I was eleven years old. It's stopping me from doing my best at uni. I need to get a grip of it."

As I talk, he nods. This is definitely good practice for talking to a counsellor.

"Those tablets *are* really bad though," he says. "They…well, I didn't want to say anything, but you haven't been the same recently. When I first met you, I…" He stops and looks away from me.

"What? What is it? You can tell me." It's my turn to be concerned now. He pulls back, letting go of my hand, and I reach over towards him. I don't even think about it, my hand darts out and rests upon his arm.

"I shouldn't say anything." He shakes his head and looks back at me, his eyes meeting mine. He doesn't pull away from me.

"No, please. When you first met me, what?"

"You were…different. You were more light-hearted." He pauses again before

184

saying. "You were more *alive*."

I let my grip on his arm loosen, but I leave my hand resting on his cool skin. This hits home, and it feels like a slap. I know what the tablets did to me last time. I don't want to change like that again. I haven't had Zoe keeping an eye on me, watching out for changes. Perhaps Carl is right.

"Do you think I have changed, then? Recently, I mean?" I can hardly get the words out. My breaths are shallow and fast. This is why I need the tablets. I'm sure I need them.

"You're..." He stops again and looks deep in thought. He puts his hand on top of mine, sandwiching it between the two layers of his flesh. "You're more like a cardboard cut-out of yourself, of the girl I first met. It's like your soul has been flattened. Deadened, maybe. Look, I'm sorry, I probably shouldn't have said anything, but I saw this happen to my mum and I wanted to warn you. I wanted to stop you before you got hooked on them."

"Hooked?" I say it without thinking, but after I have spoken the word, it starts to consume me. Is that my future? Am I going to become a zombie-like addict? I don't want that. I want to be me. This is exactly what happened before. This is why I have avoided these drugs for so long.

Carl nods his head slowly, and never takes his eyes off mine.

"I think you can do this without the tablets, Violet. I know that you are stronger than you think you are."

I haven't been. Not so far. I have tried, and there have been good patches, but on the whole, I am anxiety's slave. It can do whatever it wants with me - and it does. I want to get up and leave. I need the toilet. I think I do, anyway, perhaps my body is just telling me that so that I have an excuse to run away. I want to be away from this conversation. I can't do this.

"I can't," I say.

He pats my hand softly. It should feel condescending or patronising, but strangely it doesn't.

"Really, you can. You are so full of life and energy, usually. Isn't that who you want to be? What good is it getting over your anxiety if the result is this?"

I didn't realise that I was so bad, that

I was so useless now. He must see it. He lives with me. He sees me every day.

"I shouldn't have said anything," he says, suddenly pulling away again.

He sits back in his chair and I get a strange sensation of feeling too far away from him. It's disconcerting how these thoughts enter my mind without any conscious decision on my part.

"I'm sorry. I was out of line," he says. "It's nothing to do with me."

"No. No. It's fine. Really." I want to reach over and pull his arm back, for some reason, the physical contact between us felt good. I don't know why. It was somehow grounding me, I think. I felt like we were connecting, that he was listening, that he was actually interested in me. "I'm glad you said what you did. I would never have noticed the change in myself."

"And Zoe is wrapped up in Luke now," he says, echoing the thought that I had earlier.

I nod in acknowledgement.

"I tried the drugs before. Not these exact ones, different ones. When I was younger." I'm speaking in rapid, short snatches; my breathing pattern is still too fast and too light. "It did what you said. It changed me. I was scared. I mean, I haven't tried them again until now because I was scared."

"You don't need them," he says again. "You should be you, not the person that the tablets turn you into."

"I'm on the waiting list for counselling," I say. It sounds defensive, I know as the words come out.

"So that you can sit and talk to someone for an hour every week about how terrible life is?" He snorts a short, sharp laugh. "It's no good, Violet. You don't need that."

"What else do I have? I have to get on top of this. My course means so much to me, and I can't keep messing up because of my anxiety."

"Have you messed up though? Have you really?"

"You weren't here last year. I had this exam, a really important exam, and I couldn't even start it. I ran away before it even really began."

"And you think it was your anxiety?"

I stop dead in my tracks. Of course it was anxiety. What else could it be?

"Well..."

He tilts his head and looks at me. "Are you anxious when you are on your placements?"

"Uh, no. I know what I'm doing then. I get on with it and -"

"You get on with it," he echoes. "How about if you tried to do that in your exams? When you're feeling anxious, push those thoughts away and get on with it."

He has obviously never had an anxiety attack. I wish I had the words to explain to him that it is not as easy as he is making it out to be, but I don't know where to start.

"What's the next thing that you are going to do that you are feeling anxious about?"

"I have a pharmacology exam, two weeks from now."

"Okay, so how about you revise for your exam, make sure you know everything there is to know, and if you start to feel anxious, come and talk to me. Let me help you through this. I know that you must have relied on Zoe before but she's not here for you right now…"

"She's always here for me," I protest, without arguing about the other suggestions he has made.

"She's not available for you all the time now," he says, without backing down. "I want to help you. I want you to stop taking those evil tablets."

"They could help me," I say, but I already know that I have to stop. If they are creating such a change in me that Carl has noticed, they must be bad.

"Try it? For me?"

"Why would you even want to do this? Why do you want to help me? Because of your mum?"

He nods but stops himself. "That, yes, but also, I like you. I like the person that you were, and I don't want her to go away. I don't want that fun, vibrant, exciting girl to get lost."

The blush is rising to my cheeks again. I don't know what to say. He is trying to lock eyes with me again, but I turn my head.

Carl reaches across the table and puts

two fingers gently upon my cheek. He tilts it in his direction, making me look at him.

"I like you. I mean it. I want to do this."

I don't know what I want, and right now, I don't know what I feel.

Chapter Twenty-Two

The pharmacology exam is on Monday afternoon, bang in the middle of my placement block. It feels weird going back in for the day, but I'm used to arranging my Monday shifts so that I can have my meetings with Zoe. The exam is at two, so I should be finished in plenty of time to get to Blackheath's and meet her.

I ought to be worrying about the exam, but I'm not. I'm thinking about seeing Zoe, talking to her about my meds, and about Carl. I've revised well for the exam, thanks to having a lot of time alone in my room. Not that I can't sit in the living room with Zoe and Luke, but even if Carl doesn't mind being a gooseberry, it still doesn't feel right to me.

Carl. I've thought about him a lot since our talk. He's been more supportive than I could possibly have imagined, but is there more to it than that? When he touched my face, it felt like there might be something else. I'm not sure. I'm probably reading too much into it. A man does something nice for me, and my brain starts imagining all sorts of things.

I will be glad to have this exam behind me, and out of the way. If I pass, that is. Last year when I failed my first OSCE, I felt like it was hanging over me the whole time between the failed attempt and the resit. It was like a constant pressure weighing down upon me. I don't want to feel like that again. This year's OSCE is a week away. I can't start thinking about that now though.

Despite having stopped the tablets, I don't feel as anxious as I thought I was going to. I walk into the room, I take my place in my seat, and I look ahead to the screen at the front. I want to clear my mind. I don't want to think about anything. As long as I don't clear everything that I have learned about pharmacology and drug calculations, I'm going to be fine.

Twenty-three students sit at twenty-three desks. In front of each of us are a few sheets of paper, and an examination question sheet. We had to drop our bags by the entrance, only calculators and pencils are allowed on our desks. As soon as I look down at the paper, I have to put my hands onto my knees. I'm trying to keep them from trembling; I can already feel how clammy they are.

It's begun. I should have known that I wasn't going to get away from my anxiety that easily. I'm worried that my pencil is going to slip straight out of my fingers and roll across the floor. Now my head is filled with numbers, equations, drug names, and everything that I have been practicing to help me to pass this exam. I need water, but we weren't allowed to bring our drinks in. I can't go back to my bag. I'm on the verge of putting up my hand, calling the supervisor over and asking to be excused. I'm burning up, I can feel it. I should have sat near the door. If I have to run, everyone is going to see me.

I take a few breaths and look straight ahead to the front of the room. I fix my attention on the supervisor. I try to focus all of my thoughts onto what she is saying. She runs through the procedure for the examination. Thirty minutes. Answer every question. Pass mark is one hundred percent. I don't need reminding.

I know that today I have to get

everything right. I want to keep looking at the supervisor, but I can hear Ashley breathing to my right. She sounds almost as nervous as I am. I turn my head slightly, and she looks back at me. Her mouth forms a tiny smile, and I know that she is trying to reassure me, even though she feels awful herself. I move my hand slightly into view from under the desk and give her a thumbs up gesture. Good luck. Good luck to both of us.

"Turn your papers over," the supervisor says. All around the room a wave of noise ripples. The tapping of pencils being picked up and the swoosh of papers being flipped and placed onto tables. I'm probably the last to look at the questions. I take my time, not because I don't think I need every moment that I have allocated to me, but more because I don't want to drop my paper or my pencil onto the floor. My nerves are on edge, and it seems highly likely that I'm going to do something stupid.

I look at the writing on the sheet. There are a series of calculations, and some questions that I have to write out answers for. Before I even start, I turn on my calculator, distracting my mind from the thought of having to actually work on the answers for as long as possible. I look back to the sheet. I know how to do this. I can do it.

I tap the numbers I need into the calculator. I had to buy it especially for the test, we aren't allowed to use the apps on our phones. It feels almost archaic to use these big-buttoned pieces of equipment. Still, I know that on the wards the same technology will be right there by the drug cupboard when I need it. I don't have to get my maths completely right, but I do have to know how to make the calculations so that the calculator gets the maths right. Out in practice lives will depend on whether we work out the correct dosage.

I feel my anxiety nip away at me, and I try to push ahead. I felt it last night before I tried to sleep. I felt it this morning when my alarm blared out, and I hit the snooze button. I felt it on the walk into uni. I felt it when I was standing in the corridor, trying to appear like I was listening to Simon and Sophie talking about their weekends. I feel it.

Sometimes anxiety hits me like a truck. It slams into me, pushes my heartrate out of control, makes me feel like I can't breathe. Sometimes it's like drowning, as though I am thrashing my arms and legs about, trying to get to the surface, but my thoughts keep pulling me further and further down.

Today, every time the thought tries to enter my head "you can't do this" or "you're going to fail", I say "no". I try to tell that voice that it's time to shut up, because the voice has spoken to me and held me down for too long.

I don't know. I don't believe it can be this easy. After all this time, I can't simply shut up the internal voice that I have come to believe, no matter how bad it has made me feel. Somewhere else though I hear Carl's voice. I hear him telling me that I can succeed. I hear him describe the girl that I was without the meds, the girl that I want to be. When I'm on placements I never worry - why do I need to feel anxious now.

"You don't," I hear Carl-inside-my-head tell me.

Someone who barely knows me

believes in me. Someone likes me.

Whichever one of those facts is driving me on, it is working. I look down at the paper again, and I smile.

I know this. I can do it.

Chapter Twenty-Three

With Zoe on placements, I miss our morning walks into uni together, and walking into town to meet her after my exam gives me too much thinking time. I start with the basics, wondering if I screwed up the exam, and if so, how badly. If I did, I did. It doesn't actually matter how much I screwed up this time. If I even got one thing wrong, I would have to resit. Strangely that thought helps me to focus and calm my mind. For the second half of the walk I'm consumed with what I'm going to say about Carl.

I'm not concentrating, and I almost trip over a dog lead that's trailing between a short squat sausage dog and the short squat man who is walking him. I don't wait for the man to chastise me. I mutter *"sorry"* under my breath and carry on.

If I talk to Zoe about Carl, and how my thoughts on him are changing, I will also have to tell her about stopping my anxiety meds, and she's not going to be pleased. It's my life, and my decision though. Maybe it's better if I don't say anything.

Zoe is already sitting at our usual table when I arrive. There are two cups on the table. I know one will have her extra-hot-extra-shot mocha, and one will hold my latte. Some things never change.

We make small talk for a while, while I dance around the things I really want to talk about. The fact is I don't want to talk about the important issues at all. I want to relax and enjoy being with my friend.

I think I have escaped, until Zoe returns from the counter with our second round of coffees.

"Now are you ready to talk to me about whatever's on your mind?" she says, without any trace of judgement.

I'm taken off guard, but I think quickly. "I have my OSCE next week."

It's the truth. It's not what has been on my mind, but it is the truth. In a few days from now I will have my OSCE, the scenario-based assessment that I have to pass to make it through to the next year of the course. Having failed on my first attempt last year, well, okay, having run out of the room before I had a chance to see if I could even pass, it would be understandable if I were terrified, especially with my crappy anxiety, but that's not how I actually feel.

I thought I would be dreading the OSCE. In reality, I feel strangely calm and resigned. I'm not used to feeling this way. I expected the sweats, the nausea, the inability to act. I expected to be chewing my nails off, but instead, I'm focussing on preparing and performing. I managed it for the pharmacology exam, I can do it again.

"Do you need me to run through scenarios with you?" Zoe says. Her face is full of concern. She knows how much this means to me.

I remember how she and Luke helped me last year. Him as a make-believe patient, and Zoe as a stand-in assessor. It seems that so much has changed over the past twelve months.

"I'm meeting up with Simon and the girls on Sunday afternoon," I tell her.

I made plans because I thought that she would be busy with Luke, but instead of looking relieved, a look of hurt flashes across her face.

"Oh," she says. "Okay. I could have,

I mean, I would have...I'm happy to help, if you need me."

I nod and try to smile. "I know," I say. "I just thought, I didn't want to, I -"

This is what it has come to, the two of us speaking in broken sentences to each other, tiptoeing around each other's feelings.

"Really," I say. "It's fine."

"I suppose they want to practice too," Zoe says. I don't know if she is trying to make *me* feel better, or herself.

"Yeah," I say. "We are like a little study group. And actually, I don't feel as bad this year."

"Probably the tablets. They must be working."

"Uh, yeah. I suppose they must." I should probably tell her.

I was wrong. *This* is what it has come to, and this is not what I want.

"Actually, I'm not taking them. I stopped."

Her eyes widen, and her mouth drops slightly open.

"I'm sorry, I don't know why I didn't tell you. I should have talked to you, but -" I don't want to say it. I don't want to

202

make her feel bad about being with Luke and not me. I bite my tongue and leave the sentence hanging.

"Right," she says. "Are you sure?"

"I feel fine. I had my pharma exam and apart from a few seconds of the sweaty palms I was fine. That's normal. Everyone feels like that."

"You don't have to get defensive. It's fine. I'm glad you're feeling better." She pauses before saying, "You didn't go for the counselling either then? Are you still on the list?"

"No. I mean, I haven't been. I don't think I'm going to go. My name is still on the list. It could take some time, so…I suppose it's my safety net."

"Won't they want you to have been taking the drugs that you were prescribed though? Do you not think you -" She stops and presses her lips together tightly. "Whatever you think is best, Vi. I'm just worried about you, that's all." She picks up her spoon and starts to swipe it through the chocolatey foam at the bottom of her mug, as though she isn't able to look at me anymore.

203

I look forward to our chats every week, but this time the atmosphere is tense and tight, almost claustrophobic. But this is us, this is me and Zoe. How can we feel like this?

"Want anything else?" I ask, gesturing to the counter.

It's quiet in here; we are the only people in the coffee shop apart from a lady with a small white fluffy dog who is sitting in the window alcove. Her dog is on a little red pillow that the owner must carry around everywhere with her. Most days, I would nudge Zoe and point at the pup, and we would coo over it. The fact that we are not doing that thuds heavily in my chest.

"Thanks. I shouldn't, but…okay," she says.

For a second I want to smile, knowing that we will have more time together while we drink more coffee, but as I start to stand up, she pulls out her phone and looks at the time. Just that simple movement is enough to make me painfully aware of how limited our time together now is.

I know that I have to get used to this.

It's ridiculous having these feelings of loss and wanting to be with her, when all that she is doing is having a normal life. Without realising it, over the years I have become completely dependent on Zoe. Now I'm trying to balance my need for her time with my need to become independent. I'm sure I shouldn't feel bad about reaching out to my other friends - my course mates - for help with my revision, but for some reason, I do.

The rest of our coffee date passes in a subdued shimmer. I feel like we are skimming the surface of everything that we talk about, rather than actually discussing anything real. I avoid talking about my emotions, and for her part, Zoe steers clear of the subject of Luke. As these are the two main drivers in our lives at the moment, what results is a tepid, over-polite conversation that leaves me feeling empty.

Of course, I don't mention Carl.

We walk back to Tangiers Court through the park and arrive home to find Luke and Carl in the living room together, deep in conversation. I never considered that either Luke or Zoe spoke to Carl much -

mainly because all their time is devoted to each other - but then I never stopped to wonder what Luke does on a Monday when Zoe and I have our coffee date.

"Okay guys?" Zoe grins.

She throws her coat over the back of the sofa and bends down to kiss Luke.

The change in her mood as soon as she sees him is palpable. It's not as though she was unhappy, spending time with me, but now that she is with Luke, she is glowing, back to her usual happy self. Instead of feeling put out by this, I stand in the doorway, looking at the two of them. His face is all smiles and he reaches up to embrace her, pulling her towards him, down onto the sofa by his side.

I want to be alone. Not to be out of their way, leaving them to each other's company, not that. Carl is here anyway, so it's not as though they have the place to themselves. I need some time to think.

"I'll just -" I move backwards slightly, stepping into the corridor.

"We were about to watch Salvage Den," Carl says. "Come and sit down. Don't leave me here being a gooseberry."

He has sat with the two of them often enough for me to know that he doesn't really have any concerns about being a third wheel. The look in his eye tells me that he wants me to stay. He moves his head ever so slightly, indicating that I should do as he suggests.

I can't think of a decent reason why I shouldn't, so I drop my bag in the hallway, throw my jacket over the bottom of the bannister, and go back into the living room to sit beside Carl.

Things are different now. I have to accept that. I can sit in my room on my own all evening or I can be here, with my friends, and start getting used to it.

Chapter Twenty-Four

Although I'm on placement for the rest of the week, I feel like I can't concentrate on what I'm doing. All I can think about is the upcoming OSCE. I'm on the antenatal ward, and some of the scenarios are linked to antenatal care and pregnancy-related problems, so I'm trying to see my shifts as revision. I suppose it should always be this way. Everything I learn in class is designed to help me to be a better midwife when I'm on my placements. Everything I learn in placements must be able to help me do better in my assessments.

I don't have to worry about feeling bad at home, shutting myself in my room and going over and over the flashcards that I have written out. Zoe knows what happened last year, and so does Luke. They know how important it is that I pass this exam, for my course and for my own confidence. I cram and I cram. Occasionally Zoe brings a mug of tea and a couple of biscuits up to my room, and gives me an encouraging smile, but apart from that I'm completely absorbed in my revision.

The study session with my course mates is one last push to help me to stuff everything I possibly can into my brain. We spend the whole day running through every scenario, and it's reassuring to me that I seem to remember just as much as any of them do. I don't feel stupid. I don't feel like I can't do it. I feel normal. That's kind of a big deal for me.

On Sunday evening, when I get back from meeting Ash, Simon and Sophie, my plan is to put the books away and chill. I'm in my pyjamas by nine o'clock, acutely conscious that my exam is in twelve hours' time.

I've stripped my make-up, which doesn't take long as I barely wear more than foundation and mascara, and I'm smearing moisturiser onto my face when there's a quiet, short tap on my door.

I know before I say anything that it must be Carl. Zoe would just come in, and Luke would send Zoe if he needed me. That's just the way it is.

"Hang on," I say.

I have three big smudges of thick

cream on my face, ready to be massaged into my skin: one on my forehead and one on each cheek. I can't let him see me like this. I reach for the nearest item I can and wipe my face over. My new Zara smock. I hope the cream doesn't stain.

I take a quick look in the mirror. My hair is pinned up in a bun, which I only ever do when I'm putting on or taking off my make-up, and my face looks pale and puffy.

"Er, I'm in bed," I call. I don't want him to see me like this.

"It doesn't sound like you're in bed," he says, with laughter in his voice.

I frantically unravel my bun and straighten my hair down with both hands as I stumble to the door. This is not a good look.

Carl doesn't look at all shocked or put out by my appearance.

I wave my hand at my face. "I was almost in bed. Getting ready for bed," I say, as an apology for my appearance, and for my lie.

"Okay," he says, giving me a look of amused puzzlement. "Zoe said you have an important exam tomorrow."

I nod. I have barely spoken to Carl this week. All I have thought about is the OSCE. I should probably have made time to chat with him, but –

"I wanted to say good luck. I'm sure you don't need it, but, well, you know."

Sometimes he comes across as confident and cocky, but sometimes, like now, he appears nervous, shy even. He has come up specially, to talk to me, and I should be grateful rather than being worried that my hair is a mess and my skin is blotchy.

"Thanks, Carl. That means a lot. I really appreciate it." It sounds over-the-top as I say it, but he grins anyway.

"You all set? Know everything you need to know?"

We are hovering on the landing, him outside the door, and me within the threshold of my room. I feel like I should invite him in, but something is holding me back. I need to get to sleep soon, even at this early hour. I want to give myself every chance to pass the OSCE first time.

"I think so," I say. "I've studied hard, and I know everything I can know.

Whether that's everything I need to know, well, I'll find out tomorrow."

"You are going to be fine," he says. "Better than fine. I know it. You're doing okay, aren't you?"

I know that he means the anxiety and not the studying.

"I am. Thanks, Carl."

"I knew it. You didn't need those drugs, you just needed to believe in yourself. I'm right aren't I? I was right."

There's a wave of excitement in his expression that makes him look like a child who knew the answer to an important question. It's really quite sweet.

"You were," I smile. "I really appreciate it. I'm sorry I haven't had much time –"

He shakes his head and cuts me off.

"It's fine, really. I know you have had studying to do."

I turn my head, looking into my room and wondering again whether I should invite him in. I'm only thinking about the two of us sitting down to talk, rather than standing here, but there still seems something wrong about having him in my

212

room with me.

He must have noticed me looking, because he says, "I'll leave you to get to sleep now. I'm sorry I interrupted you."

"Thanks. And thanks for coming up. Things will be back to normal after the exam. I'll be downstairs more often."

He smiles again, his blue eyes shimmering. "I'll look forward to it. You'll smash it tomorrow. You can do it. I know you can."

I almost reach out and hug him, but I stop myself. Instead I step backwards into my room and wait for him to turn and walk down the stairs before I close my door.

I haven't had time to think about Carl, or about what might happen, everything has been about my exam. Still, he has had time to think about me and he thinks that I can pass.

A warm glow courses through me, and any tension I had left about tomorrow's OSCE slides away. I know everything I need to know. What is there to worry about?

Despite my increased confidence, this year's OSCE scenarios are going to be tougher than those I faced last year. I have had two experiences of doing this before, thanks to my resit, so I have to see that as a positive.

I have memorised every intricate detail. I know the scenarios inside out. I know that all of this will count for nothing if my anxiety overwhelms me again.

I try to focus on the image that fills my head - Carl telling me that I can do it. I picture myself back out in the garden, sitting in front of him, my hands in his, listening to him say that I'm clever and competent. All I need to do is believe in myself the way that he believes in me. Something about the way he talks to me, building me up the way he does, makes me feel a something that I can't describe. He's a good friend, that's what it is. I have only ever felt that warmth from being with Zoe before.

No matter how well prepared I am, the echoes of last year are reverberating through my mind, shaking my confidence, making my thoughts turn to swirling images, rather than the sharp focus I need. Still, I'm more determined than anxious, and every time the negative ideas spill into my brain, I try to replace them with positives.

"Violet," Zita calls me into the lab.

"You can do it," I hear Carl's voice. It's clearer than my own self-doubt. The words are sharp in my memory, and I tune into them. I can do it. I'm not going to bottle it this time, I'm going to ace it.

I fix Zita with a confident smile and I walk into the lab.

Chapter Twenty-Five

With my OSCE behind me, the rest of the term starts to race by. On the morning of my SPOKE day with Helen, the specialist mental health midwife, she picks me up from home to take me out for whatever it is she has planned. In a way, this feels a lot like my community placement last year. We are sitting in Helen's car, going to visit women, in the same way that Stacey and I went last year when I started my course. It feels comfortable and known in a way, but I also know that today is going to be different.

"This morning we will go into the Linden Unit. There's just one lady in the mother and baby unit at the moment. She's been there a couple of weeks, and she's a lot better than she was, but…" She leaves the sentence dangling, and my mind tries to put together the rest of the words.

"There are two visits this afternoon," Helen says. "I try not to book any more than that, because I never know how long I'm going to be staying with any particular woman. I want to give all the time that any woman needs. Sometimes it's a brief visit, sometimes I will be there for hours."

I nod. I have no idea what to expect from these appointments.

"They won't mind having me along?"

"The ladies we're going to visit today know you're coming, and they're fine with that."

Helen doesn't wear the uniform that the other community midwives do. She's in plain clothes: a smart dark blue skirt and a navy and white striped tunic. I feel conscious of my uniform, but I know that I need to be recognisable as a student. Especially when we go into the mother and baby unit; I don't want to be mistaken for a member of staff and asked to do things that I have neither the knowledge nor experience to tackle.

The Linden Unit is a fifteen-minute drive out of town. I imagine the building has been a mental health hospital for many years. It's an old-fashioned building, a stark contrast to the modern styling of St. Jude's where I have my placements. Despite being a staff member, who must visit the unit on a semi-regular basis, Helen buzzes to be let into the ward. She says her name and adds mine as an afterthought. She looks up at the camera mounted above the door, as if to confirm that she's telling the truth about who she is. I'm used to working on wards where security is paramount, so it comes as no surprise. There's a sharp buzz, and the lock is released.

Inside, there's a corridor, much the same as any other corridor in any other ward, with side rooms off to the left and right. Just before the nurses' office I can see what looks like a drug treatment room. There's a woman in the corridor, turning into a room as we walk along. The staff wear plain clothes; without knowing anyone, and not being able to see a name badge from here, the woman could be a nurse or a patient. I'm already unsteady about being on here, and the thought of not knowing who's who throws me further off balance.

Helen pops her head into a small square room where two nurses are sitting. At least I assume they are nurses.

"Hi. This is Violet. Student midwife.

218

She's with me today, okay."

"Alright," says a chubby man in a sweatshirt and trousers combo. "Just going to see Meg?"

"Unless you have anything I need to know about?"

He shuffles through a large diary, then looks up and shakes his head. "No, nothing new. Did you come in yesterday?"

"Briefly, yes."

He nods, and mumbles through Meg's progress over the past twenty-four hours. I can feel my own anxiety rising. I'm starting to wonder whether it was such a good idea to come here. I can't try to avoid caring for women with mental health disorders just because I can't handle my own though. I have to get a grip. I have the swimming buzz of nausea and I know that if I don't get out of this room and get some air soon I'm likely to have my first major anxiety attack of the year. I was stupid to stop the meds. I was getting somewhere, I was -

"Are you ok, Violet?" Helen asks, putting her hand instinctively onto my wrist. I think she is trying to steady me, but then I realise that she is checking my pulse.

"Oh, yes. Yes I am. I'm fine. Sorry. I skipped breakfast. I'm just feeling a bit…you know."

She looks at me as if she doesn't know but accepts my answer.

"Okay. If you need to sit down, or get a drink or whatever, let me know."

I'm making a fool of myself in front of Helen and these two nurses. I have to snap out of it before I get to the patient.

I can feel my heart threatening to switch up to triple time, that familiar thumping in my temples and the churning of my gut. I was expecting this. I knew I would feel anxious here, the only surprise to me is that it has taken this long.

"Sorry," I whisper. "I'm fine, really."

Helen eyes me cautiously but turns to finish her conversation with the mental health nurse. By the time she is ready to go and see the patient, I have managed to settle myself sufficiently to tag along.

She bumbles ahead of me, giving me a brief tour of the ward as we walk. It doesn't look much different to the delivery suite, with its side rooms and lino corridors. There aren't any patients in sight, but I can hear a baby crying somewhere further down, in one of the rooms.

"We have space for women that have pre-existing mental health conditions and need extra support after childbirth, and we have patients admitted with postnatal psychosis, that kind of thing."

That kind of thing. Of course.

"There's just one lady here at the moment?" I ask.

"She has her baby with her, but the nurses who work in the mother and baby unit are there to monitor and support her."

I've met a couple of women with postnatal depression, it's a surprisingly common occurrence. I've never encountered anyone with any other mental health disorders though, not yet. Something about supporting women who have psychological needs...I suppose I can identify with it. I've had my own demons to fight for years. I have tried to do it by myself, I know what that is like. I know how it feels to not want to be labelled, to not reach out for help when I have really needed it.

221

When we get to Meg's room it is empty. For some reason, a feeling of panic kicks in. I think she has taken the baby and escaped. It's a ridiculous thought to have. Meg is a voluntary patient here; she wanted to be admitted, and she wants to receive support. I know nothing about her, and I have somehow made an assumption about her. It reminds me even more clearly about how I expect people would make assumptions about me if I told everyone about my own mental health issues. If I jump to these ridiculous conclusions, having battled my own issues, how can I expect other people to hold back their judgment?

"She's probably out in the garden," Helen says, calmly, as though this is a regular occurrence. She isn't at all concerned about Meg's absence. I shouldn't be either.

True enough, we make our way out to the small quad, enclosed between the blocks of the hospital, but apart from that a pretty, green, airy space, and find Meg sitting in the shade with her pram. The baby is sleeping, and Meg is absorbed in a book.

I don't know what I expected, but

Meg appears completely normal. There's nothing remarkable about her manner or the way that she talks to us. Helen chats to her about the baby, the book, and life in general. It doesn't feel like we are doing anything clinical, and essentially we are not. The mental health nurses are providing Meg with the care she needs to recover. Helen is checking in, seeing what additional support is needed. Meg appears open and unguarded, and I can tell that the relationship that Helen has built up with her is strong and trusting.

We sit with Meg for just over an hour, until one of the nurses pops their head into the garden to let her know it is time for a session to begin. Again, I make the mental connection that it must be a therapy session, and again I'm wrong. It is baby massage. I have so much to learn about maternal mental health, and how to support women. I have so much to learn about the way that I leap to conclusions. I would never have come here if it were not for the SPOKE placements; I would never have experienced this. I'm already glad that I made this choice.

On the way back to town for our two

afternoon visits, Helen tells me how lucky Meg is. The mother and baby centre at the Linden Unit is one of only seventeen in the country. I can't quite believe it. So many women experience some mental health issues in the perinatal period, I can't believe that these units aren't more widely available.

"Most places are lucky to even have a specialist midwife," she tells me.

"What happens in the other towns? What happens if there aren't any units, or specialists?"

"Then they are cared for by their regular midwifery teams, and whatever mental health services are available locally. If women need to be admitted, unfortunately a lot of the time that means separating them from their babies."

I shake my head. I can't believe that something so basic is so difficult for women to access. I suppose that mental health services in general can mean a long wait, just like the list I'm on for my sessions. I should take my name off the list, let someone else move up it. I can do this on my own.

For some reason, I expected both of the home visits to be with postnatal women. Even after a year and a half of training I'm green enough to think that maternal mental health means postnatal depression. The first woman that we call in to see is indeed one of the more than one in ten women that is fighting postnatal depression. Add to that all the women who go through the baby blues, and I'm surprised that I haven't already been taught about maternal mental health in more detail. I'm sure I will be. As Helen listens to the woman, exploring her feelings and giving support I feel completely out of my depth. I wouldn't know where to start.

The second visit hits me with an even greater impact. The woman that we visit is heavily pregnant. She had a stillbirth at term in her previous pregnancy and is suffering from anxiety far worse than anything I have ever experienced.

"It's a form of PTSD," Helen tells me. "The trauma from her last birth…"

I nod. She doesn't have to finish the explanation; I can put it together by myself.

"Sometimes in cases like this, women can become severely depressed.

Especially coming up to the birth, as Kaye is. I'm meeting her weekly, but if she needs more regular contact, I will be here for her."

"I can't imagine what it must feel like. Having been through that and, well –"

Now it's me that doesn't need to finish the sentence. There is a lot that is intrinsically understood between midwives, and between them and their patients.

Even with the anxiety that I have lived with, I genuinely can't imagine what Kaye is going through. Her anxiety is rooted in experience. Mine seems flimsy in comparison. What basis do I really have for being so hard on myself, and so afraid of failure?

My day with Helen has given me a lot to think about, both in terms of my developmental needs as a student midwife, and my personal mental health. I won't forget the women that I have met today. I have so much to learn about so many things. Perhaps one day I will train to be a specialist in maternal mental health. I thought the SPOKE visits were going to be a waste of time, but I have learned so much on just this one day. I understand how important it is to see the bigger picture, and now I want to learn more.

Chapter Twenty-Six

After my day with Helen I feel inspired and yet drained. All I want to do is go upstairs, flop into a hot bath and shut out the world for an hour. Or longer, if I can get away with it. My head is swimming, I feel like I'm carrying so much of the day home with me. For once I hope that Zoe and Luke are out. I want to be alone. Of course, the one time that I want solitude, as I start to run up the stairs, Zoe calls me from the living room.

"Vi!"

It sounds like a question, but I know that she recognises the sound of my feet on the stairs, just as I would recognise hers. I can't carry on and pretend that I didn't hear her, but the thought does flicker through my head. I stop on the third stair, put my hand on the bannister and turn around, not moving.

"Yeah?" I call back.

"Come in here. Don't run off!"

I know she can't see me, but I still feel bad as I roll my eyes and sigh.

"Okay. Let me get changed. Be

down in a minute."

I don't want to be in my uniform any longer than I have to. I remember when I first wore it. I felt so proud, and so excited. Now it is only reminding me of everything I have seen at work. Today was so close to home. I know that's what it was; that's why it has affected me so much. I'm putting my own mental health under the microscope, and what I see is difficult to deal with.

I change and slowly make my way back downstairs. My evening does not get any better when I sit with Zoe and she starts to talk to me. She tells me she has something she wanted to bring up but didn't know how to. I can't believe we have got to this point. Still, I don't know why I didn't see it coming.

It should have been obvious.

She wants to spend the Easter holidays with Luke.

Of course, she would want to be with him. I suppose a part of me took for granted that Zoe would want to go home, visit her family, and that we would have three weeks together back in Portland.

"I'll drive you back though, of course. If you want to go, I mean."

It hadn't even occurred to me that she might want me to stay here too. What do I have back home now though?

It feels awful to think that way, because what I have is my mum. I should have called her more often; I should have gone to visit her. It's half an hour's drive, so maybe an hour on the bus. I could have made the effort. Instead, I have been tied up in university, worrying about losing my closeness with Zoe, and wallowing in my anxiety. Now, going home alone would feel as though I was treating my mum as a fall-back, rather than respecting her for what she is. We were so close over the past few years, brought together by her and my dad falling apart. What happened?

"I'll think about it," I say. "I assumed I would be going home, but -" I shrug. "If you want me to stay...?"

"I want to be here, and I don't want to be without you," she says. "You're not cross with me, are you?"

"Cross? Uh, no. Not cross."

"Something then? What?"

230

"It's a surprise, that's all. I haven't thought about it. I hadn't thought about it, I mean."

There's a frostiness between us that I have never felt before. The two of us, at odds with each other. We are adults, young adults, maybe, but adults. Of course, one of us was eventually going to have an adult relationship, and of course it was most likely to be Zoe.

"I'm sorry," she says. "I should have thought it through. I didn't even think about the impact it might have on you. I'm stupid,"

"No. You're not. We have never been in a situation like this before, that's all. The boyfriends we have had before, they weren't serious."

"You thought Jared was The One at the time," she smiles.

I did, but I was sixteen. What did I know? What do I know now?

"I know now that he wasn't. Maybe Luke is your 'One' though. If he is then I want you to be happy. I don't want to be holding you back or stopping you from doing all the things that normal people do in normal relationships. Everyone in your situation would do exactly what you're doing. It's only because you have a ridiculous clingy friend who has nothing else in her life that it's even an issue."

She looks horrified. I didn't realise that my words would have such an impact upon her.

"Is that what you really think? Because I don't think that. You're not clingy. Up until a few months ago it was you and me against the world. If it had been the other way round, if you had met someone, I'm sure I would have had just as much trouble adjusting. It's not you. It's nothing you have done, and it is nothing to do with the person you are. Tell me that you know that."

The tears are welling up in my eyes, and the dam is on the verge of breaking.

"Tell me, Violet," she says, insistent, her voice brimming with emotion.

"I'm sorry," I say. "I know. I do. Listen, give me time to think about it, okay?"

She nods, moving her head as though it is heavy and painful.

232

"We can make this work," she says. "For all of us. You will never not be important to me."

I juggle the double negative for a moment. "You'll always be important to me too. And it's important to me that you are happy."

I think I already know what I'm going to do. Being at home without Zoe is going to be tough, but she needs time alone with Luke. We aren't far away. I could come up for the day, or she can come down to me. I'm sure she will, but I need to go home.

Chapter Twenty-Seven

Easter break is even more tough than I imagined it would be. I stay at home for the entire three weeks. Zoe comes down for the first weekend, to see her parents, and of course to see me. I get the bus up to our home away from home during the second week. Apart from that, we don't see each other. We carry on with the usual text messages, even more than usual considering our physical distance, but it's not the same. I thought about asking her to come for our coffee date last Monday, but it felt twee and ever so slightly emotionally manipulative. I don't know why. She's my best friend, inviting her out shouldn't feel that way.

Zoe arrives to pick me up at just after two on the Friday afternoon before term starts again. I have been packed and ready since ten in the morning. I couldn't settle. I've been pacing the living room, watching terrible daytime TV, waiting for her to come and take me back to Tangiers Court.

When I hear the triple beep of her horn, I scramble for my bag, throw my mum a hasty hug, and dash out of the house. Seeing Mum, having some down time with her has been nice, but it has made me remember how much I like living at university. I love her so much, but the two of us need the distance between us. Being in the house I grew up in, sleeping in the bedroom that once held my cot and still has my teenage posters on the wall is a weird experience.

I throw myself into Zoe's car and awkwardly reach across to hug her.

"It's not been that long," she says, her palms flat on my back, pulling me in.

"It felt like it."

"I told you I would have come sooner. You should have said."

"I had to do this. I had to have the time here alone. You understand, don't you?" I say the words, but I'm not sure if I really believe them. Did I need to be here by myself, or am I just being a martyr for her relationship?

She nods. "Sure. I think so. I kind of understand."

It's strange, heading back to Tangiers Court. I have always thought of it as home, since we moved in together, but now, I feel more like a visitor. It is Luke and Zoe's home. I don't know where that leaves me. I'm not sure about anything anymore.

Zoe is chatting away about what she has been doing during the week, and what plans she has for the weekend, but it sounds like a stream of words to me, I can't focus. My brain is too busy.

This feeling that I have of not fitting in is getting stronger the closer we get to Tangiers Court. It's a feeling of unease and unrest. I should be happy. I should be looking forward to being back, to seeing Zoe again, and to launching into the final term of the year. Instead, I feel a little lost.

"Really, are you okay?" she asks me, taking a break from her chatter.

"I don't know," I tell her. I can only be honest.

"I thought you'd be excited to come home," she says. Her eyes are focused on the road ahead, but she flicks a quick look in my direction, trying to assess me. "Are you not happy?"

I think about the question for a few seconds before answering. "It's not you,

Zoe, really it's not. But –" The thought has only just come to me, and perhaps I should have considered it for longer before blurting it out. "- I think I ought to live somewhere else next year."

I'm glad she is driving. She has to keep looking ahead, she can't give me a look of disappointment or anger, or anything. I should have waited, it's not fair of me to say what I did, not here, not like this. As the words came from my mouth though, I knew they were true. It was a snap decision, in some ways, but surely the thought must have been there, bubbling away inside my mind for it to have come out like that.

I have been dependent on Zoe for too long. I've held her back, always making demands on her time. Maybe she would have had the kind of relationship she has with Luke before now if she weren't always stuck spending her time with me. It works the other way too. Perhaps without having Zoe as a constant crutch I would have been forced to overcome my anxiety and get myself together. I can't bear to think about it that way. She has only done her best for me.

I don't blame her for caring about me, I don't blame her for loving me. Now, I think it's time that we gave each other space, and let each other go.

"I don't know what to say," she says. Her voice is quiet and hurt. "I don't want you to leave."

"I don't want to leave you either. But I have to. I was pathetically sad over the past few weeks. I should be able to spend time with my family, and with the few friends that I have back in Portland and be able to be happy. I wasn't. I missed being with you. I missed home." As soon as I say the word I correct myself. "I missed Tangiers Court; I mean. I missed there."

"It *is* your home," Zoe says. "Things have changed, I know, but it is your home. Please. I don't want this."

"I need it, Zo. I need to be stronger."

She shakes her head silently, and I can see the moisture of tears in her eyes that she is fighting to hold back. She keeps her focus on the road ahead and drives without speaking another word.

I'm grateful that our university is only a short distance from our old homes, because the silence makes every minute feel like an hour. I don't know where the thought came from, or why my stupid brain felt the urge to make me say it. It's time for a change, though. It's time for me to change. I just have to find a way to do that without losing Zoe.

Chapter Twenty-Eight

After everything that has happened this year, the final term is almost easy. All my exams are behind me; I have a reflective assignment and another essay to write this term. I am heading back to delivery suite for my placement, and I can't wait.

Over Easter I made a pact with myself that I would try to engage more with other people. I want to try talking to my course mates more often, to get to know them better and to try to be friends with them, rather than just seeing them as people who are on the same course as me.

I'm going to try to go out more, to do more things that perhaps I wouldn't have been brave enough to do before. This change isn't only down to Zoe and Luke, it's also about myself, and who I am. My anxiety is at an all-time low; I haven't had an attack in as long as I can remember. I'm getting on top of it this time, I know I am. I feel great knowing that I am doing this myself, without the drugs.

I had a moment of weakness, when I

went to see the doctor. That's all it was. I thought I couldn't cope without Zoe, but I don't need her to carry me every minute of the day.

Although I'm telling myself that I want to be more friendly so that I can have friends, I know that I have an underlying motive too. As much as I don't want to think about it, I'm not sure that I will be living with Zoe next year. Not that I don't want to, of course I do, but sometimes I feel like Andrew, the imaginary housemate that we had last year. I might as well not be around. I don't say that in entirely a self-deprecating, self-pitying way. What I mean is, I'm not needed anymore. It's a little self-pitying, I know.

A few classes into the new term I get the opportunity to make a start on my new resolution to be more sociable. When the session breaks for coffee mid-morning, I traipse along with my three course mates.

Sophie and Ashley are already deep in conversation by the time we get to the refectory.

"It's not that I don't like him,"

Ashley says, "but I don't want the same things as he does."

"He adores you," Sophie tells her.

I have no idea who they are talking about, so I stand behind them in the queue, and smile awkwardly at Simon.

"How's it going?" I ask him, for something to say.

"Yeah," he replies. "Good thanks. Glad to be back in uni."

"Oh?" I enjoy the lectures well enough, but I'd always rather be out on placement.

"Yeah," he says again. "I don't know. I'm not feeling it quite so much this year. I was so enthusiastic at the beginning."

"You were, I remember," I interrupt.

"Recently I've been finding it tough.

"The placements? What's happened?"

"Nothing specific. I don't know if it's trying to balance uni and shifts and trying to have a life, or what, but -" He shrugs, but I know what he means.

"That's exactly it," Ashley says, turning to join our conversation. Sophie has got to the counter, and she's ordering something with an extra shot of hazelnut syrup. "It feels like there is no time."

I don't have this problem. I have the opposite problem. I have too much time on my hands. I have endless evenings and weekends with no plans, no real friends (other than Zoe of course) and certainly no romantic interest. Well, maybe I do, but it's not like I have done anything about it. I suppose the grass is always greener.

Simon nods at Ashley. "Right. I've been trying to see this girl from the nursing course."

"Kayla, yeah?" Ashley says.

"That's the one. I didn't know you knew."

"We know some of the same people."

Simon and Ashley seem to have grouped off into their own conversation. My mouth has dried up, and it feels like my brain has too. I want to keep talking, but I don't know what I can add. I don't know anything. I don't have any relevant experiences to contribute.

Sophie's got her coffee now, and Ashley is next in line, leaving Simon open for conversation again. Still, I find myself standing in silence, unable to find any words. I find small talk difficult, which is strange because it comes so naturally when I am speaking to patients.

"What about you?" Simon says. "Are you seeing anyone? How are you finding it?"

Simon is a good-looking lad. He's not much taller than I am, probably around five foot eight or nine, and he has floppy blonde hair and great skin. He's not muscular, not out of shape. I've never considered him as anything other than my course mate. I would say that he is not my type, but I'm not really certain what my type is anymore. I only even think these things because he has asked whether I'm seeing anyone. It feels like an instinctive reaction. That and laughing, because that's what I do. I laugh.

"That bad, eh?" he says. "Well, plenty of time."

"I'm not really looking," I say.

"What about the hottie I saw you with in the union bar?" Sophie asks. She's cradling her mug in two hands, waiting for the rest of us to be served.

"What?" My mind goes into overdrive. When was I even in the bar? Not in a long time, that's for sure. And certainly not with any 'hottie'.

"It was a while ago. I was in with my girlfriend and some of our mates, and you were sitting at one of the little tables with a guy."

"Oh no!" I laugh again. It's a way of trying to cover my nerves, and I know it is probably irritating, but sometimes, I can't help myself. "You mean Carl. No. He's my housemate."

Having Sophie call him a 'hottie' doesn't really mean much, seeing as she is not interested in men, but I pause for a moment to consider.

"Now you're thinking about it!" Sophie nudges me, almost spilling her sweet-smelling drink in the process. "No laws against dating your housemate!" she says.

I know.

"What did I miss?" Ashley chips in. She's got a coffee in one hand and a small piece of granola bar on a plate in the other.

"Nothing," I say, turning to the barista.

I can hear Sophie and Ashley behind me, chatting and giggling. Simon has taken out his phone and he's occupying himself while the two girls gossip. The way Sophie and Ashley bounce off each other reminds me too much of how Zoe and I used to be. If I lived with the two of them, perhaps I would feel just as side-lined as I do now. It's as though I'm destined to be a puzzle piece that doesn't fit, like an extra tile that has no place of its own. I'd say this was my anxiety talking, but it doesn't feel like that. Social awkwardness, paranoia, I don't know.

I wanted to get to know my course mates better, to make more friends and try to fit in, but it's as though everyone already has their place in a group and there's nowhere left for me. Maybe I made a mistake coming here with Zoe, living with her, everything. I wanted us to fulfil our dreams together, but all of hers are coming true while I carry on sleepwalking beside her.

Chapter Twenty-Nine

All I get from trying to socialise more with my course mates is the numbing realisation that I'm not going to be asking to move in with any of them next year. Despite my best intentions, I can't bring myself to spend Saturday nights in the union bar. I'm not sure I could even face sitting in a living room with them, forcing myself into small talk every night. I want a quiet life. It would seem terribly boring to some people, I'm sure, but it's who I am. Whoever I am, I'm not afraid to be myself.

That does leave me in the unenviable position of *still* having no idea what I should do about my living arrangements.

I hadn't considered asking Carl about what he intends to do, but the subject comes up anyway. The two of us are in the living room, me curled on the sofa, and him spread across the two armchairs in a position that looks rather uncomfortable. He's concertina-folded himself in a way that manages to squeeze his butt against the side of one chair while supporting his legs on the other. Even with only the two of us in the room, the space feels full.

Apropos of nothing, he says, "Are the three of you extending the lease for another year?" He asks the question casually, not looking up from his phone.

It hits me out of the blue. My living arrangements for next year have been on my mind constantly, but he can't know that. I haven't mentioned it to him. I feel a bit weirded out by the question, but then the realisation dawns on me that he must be trying to make plans for next academic year too. It's not only me that has to work out where I'm going to live.

"Uh, I don't know. I haven't decided yet," I tell him.

"Okay." His answer sounds clipped.

"What will you do?" I ask. I know that he has a lot of friends, but I wonder who he will choose to live with. It's a genuine question, I'm not just trying to sound polite.

He shrugs and clicks his phone closed, turning to give me his full attention.

"I was wondering if you were planning to stay. I thought I would find out and decide from there."

"What?" I cough the word out before I even think. "Sorry, I mean you wanted to know whether we were staying?"

"Whether you were, yes. Whether you all were." He adds the second sentence as if he doesn't want me to think that he is particularly interested in what I, personally, am doing. It makes me think just the opposite.

"Right." I don't know what to say, and to be honest, I don't know where to look, I certainly can't look him in the eyes. Then I sigh and decide to let it all out. "I don't know what to do," I say. "I love living with Zoe, of course I do, but things have changed. They're different now. She has Luke, and well, you know how that is. I thought it might be time I moved out on my own, maybe with some of my friends."

He raises an eyebrow. He has lived with me long enough to know that I don't have a heap of friends on standby. He's gentlemanly enough not to mention it.

"It's not ideal, living with a couple. I try to get on with my own thing," he says.

I've noticed how he doesn't seem to

react to them being together. If they are hugging in the kitchen when he walks in, he walks around them, while I stand in the hallway, wondering whether I'll disturb them if I go in. If they are watching a film together, he's happy to sit in the living room with them, eating his snacks, chilling as if they were just two people. They are. Of course they are. They are still Zoe and Luke.

"I like living with you though," he says. "I like you."

I think about what Sophie said. The word "hottie" bounces around my head. Without wanting to look like I'm staring, I cast my eyes over him. He's focusing on the television, not me, even though we are having a conversation. He always seems distracted. Hot? Is he hot? He's attractive, sure. Am I attracted to him though? Everything about him tells me that I should be. He's tall, slightly muscular without being over-the-top beefy.

"Violet?"

"Sorry," I say. I'm not good at the not-looking-like-I-am-staring, it seems.

He smiles and shakes his head. I swear sometimes it feels as if he's reading my mind. I'm not sure whether I like it or not.

Whatever he is thinking, he doesn't appear fazed by my attention. He's already turned back to the television.

He *is* a good-looking guy. Good looking, caring, kind. I mean he's a bit untidy, and I haven't seen him cook a single proper meal since we have lived together, but as I'm far from perfect, I'm not in any place to demand perfection in a man. I can't believe I'm even thinking about this, especially not with him sitting across the room from me. I wanted to complete my course, focus on studying. I told Zoe right at the start of our first year that neither of us would have time for dating. Looks like I was wrong.

"I might stay," he says. "If you're planning on being here too."

I have no idea what to say. I want to get up and run out of the room. I feel like I've been put on the spot. My heart is fluttering, but not in a good way.

Or maybe it is.

Maybe I've been too caught up in myself to have noticed what's been happening. Carl has been there for me. We have got to know each other, talked, and laughed. I'm so unused to seeing the signs, I suppose I have stopped looking for them.

Could I stay here next year if Carl stays too? Would we be more than friends? Am I only considering this because Zoe has Luke, and I am alone? I'm so confused. I have no idea about the answers to any of these questions.

Chapter Thirty

My next chance to talk to Zoe doesn't come
until the following day. When I get home
from uni, I run up the stairs, determined to
discuss this with her. It's time I told her how
I feel. As I get to the landing, I can hear a
scrabbling noise from Zoe's bedroom.

"Zoe?" I say, as I get to the landing
outside her door.

"Hang on," she shouts.

Hang on? When have I ever had to
'hang on' for Zoe? What could she possibly
be doing that she has to hide from me?

"Are you okay?" I'm suddenly
worried. This is not like her. I put my hand
onto the door.

"Wait!" she calls, her voice
trembling a little as I push the door slightly.

I stop, my hand still pressed against
the wood, but not moving. I'm waiting for
her to say something else, but I don't know
what to expect. Then it hits me. I swear, I'm
so slow sometimes. I suppose it's because,
even though Zoe and Luke have been
together for six months now, I am only

rarely aware of any physical intimacy between them. It's almost as if she doesn't want to do anything in front of me, like I'm a child that she has to protect from seeing her with Luke.

"Oh. I'm sorry," I say, stepping backwards. "I didn't think. I didn't mean to interrupt –"

"You're not. It's fine." I can hear her moving around, pulling on her clothes.

"Really. I can talk to you later."

The door opens, and Zoe stands in the entrance. Her usually perfect hair is a tousled mess; she's wearing sweatpants and a t-shirt that I have never seen before. I didn't know she had any clothes that I wouldn't recognise. I stare without thinking.

"You okay?" she asks. "What's up?"

Behind her, I can see Luke standing, running his hands through his own messy mop of hair, and blushing a glowing shade of scarlet. He nods as he catches my eye, and hurries to leave.

"Don't go on my account," I say, as he squeezes past me.

"It's fine," he says. "We are – I mean, it's fine. Don't worry, Vi."

I feel terrible for having stopped them. I should have waited. Now I don't want to talk anymore. My stupid childish thoughts seem like a waste of Zoe's time.

I wanted to talk to her about Carl, see what she thinks about the two of us. I wanted to talk about next year. I've been thinking it through all day, and what I really need is Zoe's reassurance that everything is going to be okay.

It's going to be a tough year of study. I have my research project to complete, I'll be panicking over getting all the competencies in my PAD signed off, and I already know that taking the step to being a senior student is going to be tough for me.

I don't know if I can bear leaving Tangiers Court, leaving Zoe, and trying to get through all of this alone.

"Violet?"

I have been standing in the doorway, blank-faced and silent. After interrupting Zoe and Luke, the least I can do is say something.

"Sorry," I say.

She looks me over, and then reaches out toward me, taking hold of my hands.

"Come in. Sit down. Come on. It's fine."

I must look even more shell-shocked than I feel, because instead of sitting down next to me, Zoe hovers and asks, "Shall I go and get us both a brew?"

"No. Really, I'm okay. I don't know what...I don't know why I'm such an idiot."

"Oh, Violet."

With that, she does sit down next to me. I feel like this is her role in my life. She is the one who says, *"Oh, Violet"*. Whether it's in sympathy when I do something stupid, or amusement on the occasions that I'm being funny rather than plain idiotic. Zoe is my sounding board; that's why I came to talk to her, after all.

I rest my head against her shoulder, and I feel the tears start to stream from my eyes. I don't know if I was even expecting them. It's frustration as much as sadness. I don't know what is wrong with me. It's been a hard year. It's been a hard few years. And I need Zoe.

She does go to get tea, and I don't protest. While we sit on her bed drinking it, I tell her about Carl. She looks shocked, as if she had no idea that there was anything brewing between us. I can't say that I blame her. I don't think I had much of a clue either.

"You've kept that quiet," she says. "So, nothing has happened yet?"

I shake my head. "Nothing. He said that he likes me, and I turned into a tomato and sat there awkwardly for the rest of the evening not knowing what to say."

"Oh, Violet," she smiles. "You like him though."

"I hadn't thought about it," I say.

I can tell from her expression that she doesn't believe me. She raises her eyebrows and gives me that knowing grin.

"Really," I say. "I hadn't."

Her smile snaps off her face, as though something has just popped into her mind that makes it impossible for her to maintain it.

"What? What is it?" I ask.

"I hadn't even noticed. I hadn't seen anything between you. I barely know Carl, and I live with him. Just think how well we knew Luke by this time last year."

"Not as well as you wanted to," I

say, trying to lighten the tone.

"That's just it. It's not that I don't want to get to know Carl, I've just been so tied up in Luke. I haven't got to know my housemate; I haven't spent enough time with my best friend."

"Zoe, it's not your fault. You haven't done anything wrong. You have a boyfriend, and you want to be with him. That's completely normal. That's the way it should be." The mood has flipped from her trying to comfort me to quite the reverse.

"We've barely talked about your course, about how you're getting on with..."

She doesn't say the word. I know that she means my anxiety, and the fact that she can't even say it now makes me feel even worse. She was the one I could open up to, but it's true. Carl's the one I talk to now. It was Carl that told me I could beat it on my own. I've been getting on very well thank you without the drugs that Zoe would've had me keep taking.

"I'm fine," I say. "I've been absolutely fine."

She pauses for what feels like a lifetime.

"I think you should have carried on taking the tablets," she says. I'm about to speak, and she silences me. "For the long term. I mean, I think it would be better in the long term if you got some support now. Next year is going to be tough."

"Especially if I have to do that alone too," I say, without thinking.

The hurt look on her face is like a shard of glass thrust into my heart. I shouldn't have said that. One minute I tell her it's not her fault, and the next I try to guilt trip her. What has happened to us?

She clears her throat but doesn't retaliate.

"If you like Carl then tell him," she says instead. "Don't waste time like I did with Luke. He's made the first move. Don't leave him dangling, or you might lose your chance."

"Right. Yes. Thanks."

In the past we would have sat and giggled and discussed all the ins and outs, the merits, and the possibilities. Now all I get is that. *Tell him.* Things have changed so much. Perhaps it's the two of us growing up, getting older, starting to live in the adult world and have adult relationships. Perhaps we are just growing apart.

"Violet." She says my name, and looks at me, saying nothing else.

"Really," I say. "Thanks."

I don't want to be sitting here with her anymore. I don't feel like talking now. None of this is what I expected. I give her a short, polite smile and get up.

"I have a few things to do," I tell her. "Maybe see you later."

"Violet, please," she says. I shake my head and head for the door.

I don't know where I'm going, or what I am doing. All I know is that everything is changing. I don't like it, not one bit.

Chapter Thirty-One

My homelife might be a mess, but my course and my clinical practice are a welcome, pleasant relief. I've loved my placements this year, even the SPOKE days, surprisingly. They've all had their highlights, but I'm so happy to be back on delivery suite.

As soon as I push open the double doors to enter the ward, and hear the thudding of cardiotocograph monitors from within rooms, echoing out fetal heart rates, and the bustle of activity from the midwives' station in the middle of the corridor, it feels like a homecoming. It's busy, that's for certain. There are doctors, midwives, and midwifery assistants milling about purposefully, and I smile my hellos at each of them as I pass.

The chart on the wall in the midwives' office, where the names of the patients and details pertinent to their care are written, is full. Black marker pen scribbles and notes are scrawled in every box. It's busy, and there's a lot of activity behind that busyness. Some days, a full board and a full ward can still be sedate. Early labourers, women who have come a check-up because they are worried, none of them need a lot of immediate input but they need to be here. Today, it looks as though every woman who is with us needs close monitoring or one to one care.

Handover between morning and afternoon staff is long because of the number of women present, but the midwife in charge runs through it as quickly as possible. I don't pick up a hundred percent of what is said about everyone in every room, but I know that I'll get an individual handover from the midwife that my mentor and I take over from.

My mentor for this placement is Margaret, one of the older staff members, and I don't know her very well. The midwife that I worked with last year is on rotation to postnatal, and I'm gutted that I can't work with her again this time. In midwifery, we always try to provide continuity of care to our patients, and the same goes for the mentorship provided to students. Where possible, we work with the

262

same midwife. It's not always possible.

There's a woman in room two with fulminating pre-eclampsia. That's a disease of pregnancy recognisable by high-blood pressure, protein in the urine and swelling caused by fluid retention. Her blood pressure isn't responding to treatment, and they're preparing to take her into theatre for an emergency caesarean now.

"Room four is Reena Carmichael. She's been here for about half an hour. Straightforward pregnancy. Third baby. Five centimetres dilated, head's at the spines, and she's contracting every three minutes. Her membranes are intact."

"Good one for you," Margaret says, quietly, so as not to disturb handover.

I nod, but don't ask anything else until we are allocated to the woman's care, and the midwife who has been looking after Reena during the morning takes us to the side to handover personally.

"How's she doing with the pain?" I ask.

"She hasn't wanted any analgesia yet. I've shown her how to use the gas and air, and that's all she had last time, so…"

263

I nod.

"She's happy to have a student midwife, no problem," the midwife says.

Most women are perfectly willing to have a student midwife participate in their care. I don't take it personally if women refuse. It's their pregnancy, their delivery, and as much as possible, all I want is to help them to have the kind of pregnancy and delivery that they want to.

Margaret lets me take the lead as we introduce ourselves to Reena.

"I'm Violet, I'm a student midwife, and, under the supervision of Margaret, I'll be supporting you today, if that is okay with you?" I have to get better at my introductions. I always feel like I'm tripping over my words. It's as though I need time to relax and settle into being with someone.

"Fine, yes, no problem,"

Her husband nods and goes back to the task of rubbing her back. He seems to have discovered exactly the right area to apply pressure to.

I stay in the room with Reena for She's standing at the side of the early part of the shift. I know there's a lot of people rushing around outside of the door to this room, and I would rather be here, supporting Reena, than getting caught up in anything else on the ward. Even though it is busy out there, in here there's a sense of calm and serenity. Until the next contraction starts.

Before long, Reena is fully dilated and ready to give birth. She's standing by the side of the bed, and I'm crouching on the floor by her side. I can see the top of the baby's head. There's a brown, hairy, wet shape that moves closer towards me with every contraction.

I've never delivered a baby whilst the mother has been standing up before, but I'm not letting it faze me. I'm completely focused, and I know that everything is going to be fine. I love this feeling of calm and confidence that I get when I'm with women. I could almost forget that sometimes I'm consumed by anxiety. It's like I am a different person when I'm here in my uniform.

I look up at Margaret and she nods.

"Are you okay?" she mouths, and I nod back.

The delivery table is out of my reach, and Margaret lifts the sterile sheet and instruments onto the bed beside me where I can reach them.

"Do I need to lie down? I don't want to lie down. I can't. I...Another contraction. It's coming. I have to push."

"It's alright. Everything is fine. When you feel that urge to push just go with it. Keep listening to me though. In a short time, I'm going to ask you to stop pushing and try to breathe through the contraction, okay?"

She makes an immense groaning sound, and the baby's head comes closer towards me again.

"That's it. You're doing so well. Baby is nearly here. Keep going."

I'm trying to position my hands so that I can try to control the baby's head as it starts to emerge, and so I can't drop this child onto the floor. Margaret squats on the other side of Reena and puts her hand over mine.

"That's it," she says, just as I had to Reena. "You've got this."

"Uuuuurrrrrrrrrrggggggh."

"Okay Reena, stop pushing now short sharp breaths. Try to pant like a dog. Nice and slow. Don't push."

She makes tiny, restrained panting sounds, and the baby's head moves slowly and steadily forward. I have my fingers on his head, flexing it gently, guiding it out as it crowns.

"Perfect Reena, perfect. Just a little tiny push now."

She does exactly as I ask, and the baby's head pops forward. A gush of fluid comes with it and coats my left leg, but I ignore it and focus all of my attention on the delivery.

Margaret is holding a warm towel below my hands. I don't think that she doubts my ability not to drop the baby, but it's my first day back here, and this isn't the most straightforward of positions for me. It doesn't matter though. What is straightforward for me doesn't come into it. This is Reena's delivery, and I'm going to help her to have her baby in whatever position feels right to her.

With the next push, the rest of the baby spurts from Reena's body into my

267

arms. I catch the slippery wet girl in a grasping grab, messing up my top and my pants, despite wearing a disposable apron. It doesn't matter. It just doesn't matter.

Margaret lifts the towel up, and wraps it over the infant, mopping away the mucus and fluid.

"She's perfect," I say. "You were amazing, Reena."

Reena lets out a grunting noise and flops onto the bed.

It feels so natural; the whole birth feels like I have been guided by Reena and her body, and what she wanted to do. Rather than feeling scared or uncertain, it empowered me. I hope it had the same effect on her.

I'm still buzzing when I sit in the midwives' office with Margaret, writing up the notes.

"How do you feel?"

"Great," I say. "That was amazing."

She looks at me, as if examining my thoughts.

"You handled that so well."

"Thanks. There's nothing to it really, is there? I mean, the delivery is the easy part, sort of."

"In some ways it is. The skill comes in supporting the woman through labour, knowing what to look out for, how to make sure she and the baby are safe, and that she has everything she needs. The birth? Aside from making sure that the baby is born safely, uncomplicated deliveries are pretty straightforward."

"I hope they're all straightforward," I say.

"I wish they were," Margaret replies. "But they are not. You'll learn how to handle those situations though. Don't worry."

I nod. I've not actually been worrying at all. I don't feel at all anxious, and I didn't have any anxiety when I was supporting Reena's birth. I felt calm and in control. Not that I was controlling her, but that I was in control of myself. I knew what I was doing. I knew what to say, how to act and react. Everything was completely natural to me.

Whatever I am going through personally, being here, being on my placements gives me release and relief. I hope it is always this way, but at the back of my mind I have the fear that I will see things, experience things and have to deal with things that are far more difficult than anything I can yet imagine.

Today though, I'm full of confidence and enthusiasm, and I let those feelings carry me.

Chapter Thirty-Two

The atmosphere between Zoe and I hasn't improved since our chat. We're being civil with each other, but the change in our relationship is obvious to both of our housemates. I want to be able to talk to Zoe about the amazing birth, and all my experiences on delivery suite. Instead, I keep to myself and stay out of her way.

I've subscribed to a list of potential house shares from the university's accommodation office, but I haven't plucked up the courage to contact any of them yet. It feels so final, picking up the phone and arranging to go and see somewhere new.

Some of the houses are groups of students who've already spent at least a year together and are looking for someone to take up the place of a student who's left the house. I don't want to be that person. It'll be hard enough living with people I don't know, never mind trying to fit in with a gang who are already friends. The irony is not lost on me.

I'm sitting in the garden, flicking

through the list of houses when Carl comes out to join me. Nothing has changed between us yet either. It's not that I don't like him. I'm not looking for anyone or anything, and if I'm completely honest, I am not sure that I can be anyone's girlfriend in my anxious, messed up, introverted state of mind. If it's a one-off hook up that he's after that's definitely not my thing.

Because I don't know what I want, or what I'm doing, I've avoided talking to him.

"Busy?" he asks, even though he can see that I'm pretty much doing nothing.

"Looking at some house shares," I say.

I don't put my phone down. I keep scrolling, glancing up only to answer him.

"Right." There's a cool silence before he says, "Have I done something wrong?"

"Wrong? No." My short, snappy answer doesn't sound reassuring.

"You've barely spoken to me. It feels like –"

"Sorry," I interrupt.

I don't want to hear him analysing

my behaviour. I know that I've been rude, and I'm sure that if he ever did like me, he must be reconsidering. "I've been busy."

"End of term is coming up," he nods. "Have you got everything handed in? How's your placement?"

I look down at the table, gathering my thoughts, and then click my phone shut.

"It's good, thank you. It's been an easy term really." I pause, and then add, "At uni anyway."

"Not so easy at home," he says. "I know. I'm sorry."

I can't make eye contact. I'm shuffling awkwardly in my chair, feeling all of the familiar flutters of my anxiety. I knew that I would feel like this once we started to talk. That's why I have been avoiding this. I have to talk to him sometime though, so now is as good a time as any.

"Don't be sorry," I say. "I'm a mess. It's all my own fault."

"Don't say that. It's not true. Look at how far you have come in the past few months. You were so stressed and anxious, remember. You got so bad that you wanted to take drugs."

He says *'drugs'* as though he is implying that I wanted something illegal rather than the meds that Doctor Fisher prescribed. The word has its intended impact though. I was at the lowest point that I have been in years. I was. Even though things are not great now, at least I feel better than I did a few months ago. I'm feeling anxious right now, talking to Carl, but I am, in general, doing really well under the circumstances.

He reaches across and puts his hand onto mine.

"I know I shouldn't have said what I did. Last time we talked. It wasn't fair of me. I know that you have a lot going on." He is gently stroking my hand, and I'm not stopping him. I know that he is looking straight at me, but I still can't make eye contact. "I put you under pressure, and I'm sorry."

It was barely anything. He told me that he would like to live here next year if I am staying too. That could mean anything. I've tried to tell myself that I was reading too much into it, but by the way that I have been avoiding this conversation, deep down, I have always known.

I nod slightly, and he moves his hand along my arm. I'm sure he can feel the goose bumps that have sprung up, but he doesn't mention them.

"I don't want you to avoid me. I don't want you to feel like you can't talk to me. If I was wrong, if what I said was, well, if you don't feel the same way that I do, that's fine. I want you to know that. I don't expect anything from you."

He keeps talking, but his words swim around my head. The floaty feeling that is taking over my body is stress, not desire. He pulls his hand back.

"Should I go? Shall I –"

I can't speak, but I shake my head.

"Okay," he says.

I love this garden. I love what we have done to it. When we moved in, it was a dark, dingy yard. Concrete slabs, brick walls, nothing worth looking at. Zoe and I planted flowers in pots, strung fairy lights onto wooden frames on each wall. We spent hours looking through Pinterest boards for the kind of look that we wanted to recreate, and then even longer sourcing the table and chairs, adding the bird table to make the yard exactly how we had pictured it.

That was last year. That was when the two of us would sit out here every night, laughing, chatting, being best friends. It seems like a lifetime ago. Now I'm sitting here with a man that I have known for nine months, feeling anxious, wondering what I'm going to be doing this time next year, not even knowing where I'm going to be living. When did life become so complicated?

Carl doesn't leave, and he doesn't force me to speak. When I have finished wallowing in my thoughts, I finally look at him.

"I'm scared," I say. "Of everything. I'm scared of change. I'm scared of losing Zoe. I'm scared of not being good enough. I'm scared that if I get involved with you, you'll see what a mess I am."

He lets out a heavy sigh, and I think I have ruined everything. I shouldn't have spoken. I should have kept my thoughts to myself, and just given up on the whole idea of, well, of anything.

"I see you, Violet. I see who you are. And I like you. I like you the way you are."

He fixes me with his deep, dark eyes, and I can't stop myself from looking back this time. "You are human. You are only human. We all are. We all have our flaws and imperfections. I have plenty of my own, believe me. But Violet, I like you. I know that you have a lot to deal with, but I would like to be with you. I would like to be more than friends."

"That's a lot of *likes*," I joke, my voice wavering.

"I have a lot of like for you," he smiles back. "And Vi, this isn't about where you live next year. We don't have to find somewhere together; we don't have to live together or rush anything. I want to be with you on your terms, okay?"

I nod slowly. Maybe it would be better for us to live separately, date like two normal people who haven't spent a year living as we have. It doesn't seem to have done Zoe and Luke too much harm though.

"And if you want to stay here - if you want us to both stay here – that's fine with me too."

He's getting ahead of himself. I haven't even told him that I feel the same way yet. I smile as I have that thought. I do feel the same. I really do. Carl is different from other men that I have met. He knows about my anxiety; he has seen me at my low point as well as seeing the mask that I wear for other people's benefit.

Still, despite all that, he likes me the way I am.

"I like you too," I say. I say it because it is time to say it. I say it because it is true. "I have a lot of like for you too."

I do. I really do.

Chapter Thirty-Three

There are two weeks left until the end of term, and the end of the year. Two weeks of mate date Monday with Zoe. I have no idea what is going to happen next year. She will spend the summer with Luke, and I'll be at home on my own. It's too early to spend the holidays with Carl. I need to take my time, not rush things. I'll have my mum, but I'm worried that the chasm between Zoe and I will grow. If I move somewhere else next year, will I even see Zoe? I can't bear to think about that. My heart is racing and my head is throbbing as I walk towards the entrance of Blackheath's.

As I draw closer, I stop dead in my tracks. Instead of the bouncy petite redhead that I expect to see, there stands a six-foot-tall male. Luke. I am frozen, wide-eyed and wordless as he approaches.

"Hi," he says.

Even though I'm looking around him to see if she is standing there, I know already that it's useless. She isn't going to pop her head up and surprise me. She's not here. It really is just Luke.

"I know this is your date day with Zoe," he says, holding his hands up, as though he is trying to calm a frightened animal. "I'm sorry. I need to talk to you."

She must be in on this too. Somehow, he has convinced her to let him come here, or she has talked him into doing this. One way or the other – and I don't like either. I don't know whether I should be more confused or angry. This is my time with Zoe. Being on placement, I have barely seen her all week. I arranged today's shift as I do every Monday, so that I can be here for my time with my best friend. I could have worked a late, had a lie-in, but I rescheduled - for what?

Anger is taking over from confusion. It's that emotional, hurt kind of anger that fills you with heat and comes out as tears. I don't want him to see me like this. I don't want to make myself look even more of an idiot than I already do.

"Please, Violet. Don't. We need to talk. I can't let things go on the way that they have been between you and Zoe. Can we get a drink, sit down, and talk for a while? Please?"

His eyes are compassionate rather than judgmental. I almost feel like he wants to reach out and hug me, make me feel better, but he doesn't. I think for a moment *'Zoe would have'* but then I remember that Zoe must have played at least some part in him being here. He's right not to try. If he comes any closer, I will step away, or, worse still, push him away. I think it would be the last straw before I snapped. He shouldn't be here. I don't want this.

People are starting to look at us. Neither of us are raising our voices, at least not yet, but our body language and expressions are enough to draw the attention of passers-by. I expect we look like a couple having a tiff. His face is beginning to show the exasperation of someone that's running out of options. I'd say that is a fairly standard representation of a lover's fight, but I haven't had enough of them to be certain.

"Say something," he says, his voice quiet, but insistent.

His expression is pleading, but I don't know *what* I should say. I don't share his view that we *need* to talk, that's for certain. I need to talk to Zoe, that's what I need. Before I arrived at the café I was excited about seeing my best friend; all that energy has been channelled into disappointment and annoyance.

"Where's Zoe?" I ask. I sound weak and feeble, and I hate the way that the words come out. They make me feel even smaller and more self-conscious.

"She's at home," he says. "Look. You can have your date night another time this week. I need to talk to you. Okay?"

It's not okay. None of this is okay. The words *'date night'* don't sound right to me. Not right now anyway. We refer to this between ourselves as our coffee date or mate date, but hearing him call it date night makes it feel trite or even risible. Is that what Luke thinks about our meet ups? Are they a joke to him? Maybe he has never liked me. He probably thinks I'm in the way.

I should have seen this coming. He wants to tell me to get out, find my own place and give Zoe the space to live her life.

Happily.

Without me.

These thoughts run through my head, but I don't let any of the words or feelings spill out. Instead, I shrug slightly, not letting my eyes meet his. I know that if I look at him now I won't be able to hold back my tears.

We are too close to the entrance. People are pushing around us, past us, to get inside. I need to decide whether I'm staying to talk with him, or whether I should walk away before he can say things that I don't want to hear. What good will that do though? I will have to have this conversation sometime. We live together, at least for now.

A man steers his daughter, still in school uniform, past us, shaking his head at me as he squeezes by. I understand that people must wonder what we are talking about, and why we need to do it in a place that inconveniences them. A woman is trying to manoeuvre her buggy around Luke and I into the coffee shop, encumbered by the phone in her right hand. Even with both hands gripping the bar, she would still have a hard task to move around us.

I step to the side, into the shop, and it seems my decision is made. Leaving will

achieve nothing. I won't have seen Zoe
either way. She obviously agreed with Luke
that he should come here – no matter who
had the initial idea. He would never have
forced her to stay at home. He's a good
person, and they are good together.

I let out a sigh, and nod towards the
counter.

"I could manage a latte," I say.

I can almost hear my stomach
reminding me that I promised it at least one
slice of cake. Somehow I don't feel like it.
Not anymore.

Five minutes later, we are sitting opposite
each other at one of the tables near to the
window. I'm stirring my latte, watching the
coffee leak into the foam in creamy spirals.
Luke is sitting still, watching me. I can feel
his eyes on me, but I keep all of my focus
onto the tall glass mug.

Luke picks his words carefully. "I
know you've been used to spending more
time with Zoe. I know that this has been
strange for you." He pauses between each
sentence, as though they are stepping stones
that he is trying to negotiate, forming a

bridge between he and I. One wrong word and he could stumble off and be swept away. "It's strange for me too," he continues. "I don't want you to take this the wrong way –"

If there's any phrase that is bound to make me even more anxious than I already am, it is that. I look up at him, but I know that I shouldn't have. He must be able to read my apprehension. I must look so stupid.

"Zoe. You. Well, you're both adults. You have been together all of your lives, and from what Zoe has told me you have been through a lot together."

Of course she has told him things about herself. How much has she told him about me? Does Luke know everything that has ever happened in my life too? Why didn't I think about this sooner? There's nothing terrible, but I feel like my past has been invaded somehow. That anger is boiling back up within me.

"She shouldn't have told you anything," I snap.

"That's what people do, Violet," he says, his voice smooth and soothing. "This is what I mean. This is what I wanted to say.

You have to let her go. Not all of her. Not your friendship. I'm not asking you to not be friends, far from it. I want you two to always be friends. I know how much she loves you. You are amazing, the two of you together. But Vi, you need to let her live her life and have this relationship with me, and find a way to balance that with finding your own life."

Now he's saying I'm a no-life loser. Is that what it is? I look away again, trying to make sense of his words.

I have a slice of carrot cake on a plate in front of me, but I haven't eaten any of it. I take my fork, and run it along the buttercream, forming deep furrows that I'm sure match the ones on my brow. What do I want in life? Who am I without Zoe? Luke reaches across to me, and puts his hand on mine, stopping me from destroying the cake.

"That came out wrong, I'm sorry." If he was trying to get across those stepping stones before, now he is wading through the water, still trying to reach me. "I know you have other friends, other interests. You are doing a great course; being a midwife is going to be so wonderful for you. I don't

286

mean that you have no life. I mean, well, I suppose I mean that you have to do things for yourself sometimes. Zoe will always be there for you, but you need to be there for yourself too."

"That makes no sense," I say. "I'm always here for myself. I'm with myself every minute of every day."

He looks at me. "You are. But I feel like I'm taking her away from you, that she should be with you, keeping you occupied, and I shouldn't feel like that."

"So, it's about you and what you want?" I push the plate forwards to the middle of the table; I don't want it anymore.

"No. Not at all. I shouldn't have said anything, I'm sorry. I just want you to be happy. I thought I could say the right thing, but obviously I can't."

"And that's what you came here for? To tell me to get a life, and that I make you feel bad? Thanks Luke. I thought we were friends but obviously I was wrong."

He's shaking his head and I can see that he wants to say something, so I stop.

"No," he says. "That's not why I'm here. No."

"Why then? There's more?"

"I feel terrible for having said all of that now. Especially because of why I did come here. It would mean a lot to Zoe, and to me, if you would reconsider your decision to move out."

The words hang in the air like smoke after the candles on a birthday cake are blown out. I don't want them, and I don't want the cake.

"After all that you said?" I mutter. I can't quite believe him.

I'm sure now that he and Zoe must have been through this, arguing about it, to the point that she somehow got him to come here and make it look like it has all been his idea. He clearly has no reason to keep me around though.

"You can be your own person and still live with your best friend," he says. "That's what I was trying to say before. I know it didn't come out right, but I think it's important for you to have balance. You won't have that by moving out and being on your own, will you? I think you would be sad and resentful and –"

"You think you know me so well?" I

288

spit out the words. I don't mean to. I hate being like this.

He's right though. I most probably would feel that way, in a flat share somewhere with people I don't know, sitting alone in my room every night. At least I would get some studying done.

"I don't, but Zoe does. I care about you though. I want things to be right. I want you to be happy. And Zoe too, of course. She isn't the same without you. Over Easter, when you weren't here, it was like there was a piece of her missing. She was never completely at ease, never totally herself. I mean, she was still wonderful, of course, and I still adore her."

He has to say that, because he must know that whatever he says to me will get back to Zoe.

He continues, "I know that you don't want to be dependent upon her, and I understand that, but the truth is, she needs you. You need each other."

"You're right though," I say. "I should have grown out of this by now. I should be able to start out on my own rather than just being an add-on in her life. We can't live our entire lives unable to be apart for more than a few days. It's just…ridiculous." I shake my head slowly as I speak.

"It isn't. Imagine that I said to you that I didn't want to be dependent on Zoe, that I don't want to feel like I can't live without her," he says.

"It's different. You're her boyfriend. You are meant to want to be with her."

"And you are her best friend. You've been her best friend for as long as either of you can remember. What kind of boyfriend would I be to her if I didn't respect that? I saw what kind of a friendship you two had before she and I got together. I fell in love with the person that she is, and she is that person, in part, because of you." His hand is still on mine, and I'm aware of its warmth and weight.

"You want me to have my own life, but you want me to stay so that Zoe isn't unhappy, and so that you don't feel guilty?"

I can't stop myself. My mind wants to turn everything to a negative.

"We both want you to stay because you are important to us. Okay? But I can see that you are beating yourself up about this dependent-independent thing, and I think you need to do something to make yourself feel better about it. Moving out is not the answer though. Please. Reconsider. Think about it."

I think about it. I think everything through from every angle, and eventually, I come to a decision. It's the only decision I could possibly have made. When my mind is set, I wonder why it took me so long. The answer was obvious. I know what I have to do.

Chapter Thirty-Four

I've set the table, there are meatballs in ragu simmering in the slow cooker, and I've opened a bottle of mid-priced red wine. I've actually already had a most of a large glass of the wine, so it's a good thing I thought ahead and bought two bottles. In a few days I will be leaving, and I want to make sure that tonight is special. There are things that I need to say, things I should have said before now. I can't leave Tangiers Court without doing this.

I stir the pasta, trying to make sure it doesn't stick to the bottom of the pan. Admittedly, I'm not the world's best cook, but I'm putting everything I have into this.

She doesn't know, of course. I haven't told Zoe that I'm doing this. I did tell Luke though, and he and Carl are going to have a few end of term drinks together while I talk to my best friend. I have been stupid. I have blamed Zoe, not externally, sure, but I have blamed her for the chasm in our friendship. It takes two people to maintain a friendship, and I have not been playing my part either. I have wallowed in my own pit of anxiety and self-doubt, and even when Zoe has reached down to try to pull me out, I have refused to take her hand.

When I hear Zoe's key in the door, a heavy wave of apprehension sweeps through me. Am I doing the right thing? Should I have just asked her to chat with me, rather than making this mighty gesture? I feel foolish, and I panic, wanting to close the kitchen door, shut her out, pretend I'm making this dinner for myself.

"Stop it," I tell myself, out loud, under my breath. "Stop it."

I've set the table, the outside metal table that she and I chose together. The sun is still high in the sky, but I have switched the fairy lights on anyway. I want this to be magical, or at least I want to work some magic between us. I want to cast a spell that will make everything better between us. I think I know how to start.

"Zoe," I call, before she has the chance to run upstairs.

"Hi." I hear her voice, but she doesn't come through to the kitchen.

"Could you, er, can you give me a

hand with something?" I stutter.

"Sure," she says.

Her voice is not as chirpy as it once would have been with me. She would have rushed to help me no matter what. I can't think about that now. Tonight is for the future, not moping about the past.

As soon as she walks into the kitchen she lifts her head, sniffing the air.

"Smells good," she smiles. "You and Carl?"

I've hardly talked to her about him, despite this being one of the most amazing things that has happened to me. That's what really made me realise, I think. Not just Luke coming to me, talking to me on her behalf. Not just that. I would always run straight to Zoe with exciting news, and this time, I did not. I don't want a future where I don't race to tell her about everything that happens to me. We have been friends too long, and we have been too close to let go of that. I have to do my part; I have to stop being so stupid and selfish.

"I was hoping you would have dinner with me," I say. I feel so nervous asking her. There's so much at stake. I'm trying to keep the feelings of fear subdued.

She looks into the slow cooker.

"My favourite," she says. "Sneaky." Then she looks up at me and smiles. "Of course."

"Just the two of us tonight," I say. "Carl has taken Luke to the bar."

Zoe raises her eyebrows at that. "He knew you were setting this up?"

"Well, after you sent him as your envoy to Blackheath's..."

I don't want to say the wrong thing, so I stop talking.

"Thanks, Vi. This will be perfect. Shall I set the table?"

I shake my head slowly, and push open the back door, so that she can see what I have prepared. A wide smile breaks across her face, and I realise it's the first time the two of us have been happy together in way too long.

"I wanted to say sorry. I have handled everything really badly this year," I say.

"No," she replies. "You haven't. I have. It's my fault. I didn't balance things properly. I wasn't there for you. I –"

I have to stop her.

"Let's just agree that we both could have done things differently," I say. "We don't have to blame ourselves, or each other. I'm happy that you're happy. I really am."

"And I hope that you and Carl are happy too. You are…?"

I know what she is asking, without her completing the sentence.

"Together?" I shrug. "It's early days. But I like him." I have lots of likes for him. "I'm going to try not to mess things up." I grin and she smiles and shakes her head.

"Don't be like that. If you are going to give him a chance, he is very lucky. You're the best, Vi. You really are. I'm sorry I haven't told you that often enough recently."

"I'm sorry too," I say quietly.

I need to strain the pasta and dish dinner out. I could use that as an excuse to put off what I want to say next, but I don't. I take a breath and speak.

"I want to stay here with you and Luke next year. If you will have me."

"Have you? I want that more than anything!" she squeaks. "Are you sure? No,

I don't care if you're sure. Just do it. Stay. Stay with me."

Her voice is rapid, racing the words in excitement.

"I'm sure," I smile. "I am completely sure. Whatever happens next year, whatever happens ever, you are my best friend, and I don't want to be without you."

We've left the dishes on the worktop in the kitchen, and we're sitting in the last of the evening sunlight when Luke and Carl come home. It feels strange seeing the two of them walk through the door and into the garden. Luke bends to kiss Zoe, but Carl looks nervous and waits for me to stand and plant a kiss on his face.

"Did you two…you know…sort everything out?" Luke asks.

Zoe and I look at each other and nod. The shared smile reminds me of the closeness that we have always had and reminds me that I never want to lose it.

"We are great," she says. "Everything is going to be perfect."

I don't know about that. I don't know what next year is going to be like. I don't know what will happen with Carl, and

I don't know how I am going to cope with my final year of training, but what I do know is that I'm going to be here, in Tangiers Court, with my best friend.

For now, that is all that matters.

Dear Reader,

Thank you for reading **"Love Lessons"**, book two in the **"Lessons of a Student Midwife"** series.

If you have enjoyed this book, please consider leaving a review on Amazon and/or Goodreads. Reviews help readers to discover books, and help authors to find new readers. It would mean a lot to me if you would take a few minutes to leave a review.

If you would like to find out more about new releases and special offers, including information about the rest of this series, please sign up to my mailing list. I'm currently giving away a free full-length to everyone who signs up.

Visit **jerowney.com** for details.

Best wishes
    J.E. Rowney

Printed in Great Britain
by Amazon

56876495R00173